FOLLOWING THE GRASS

FOLLOWING THE GRASS

HARRY SINCLAIR DRAGO

M. EVANS
Essex, Connecticut

Published by M. Evans
An imprint of The Globe Pequot Publishing Group, Inc.
64 South Main Street
Essex, CT 06426
www.globepequot.com

British Library Cataloguing in Publication Information Available

Library of Congress Cataloging-in-Publication Data

Library of Congress Control Number: 2014940370

ISBN: 978-1-59077-428-1 (pbk.)
ISBN: 978-1-59077-429-8 (electronic)

TO

MY OWN THREE

WINNIE, BARBARA AND TOM

CONTENTS

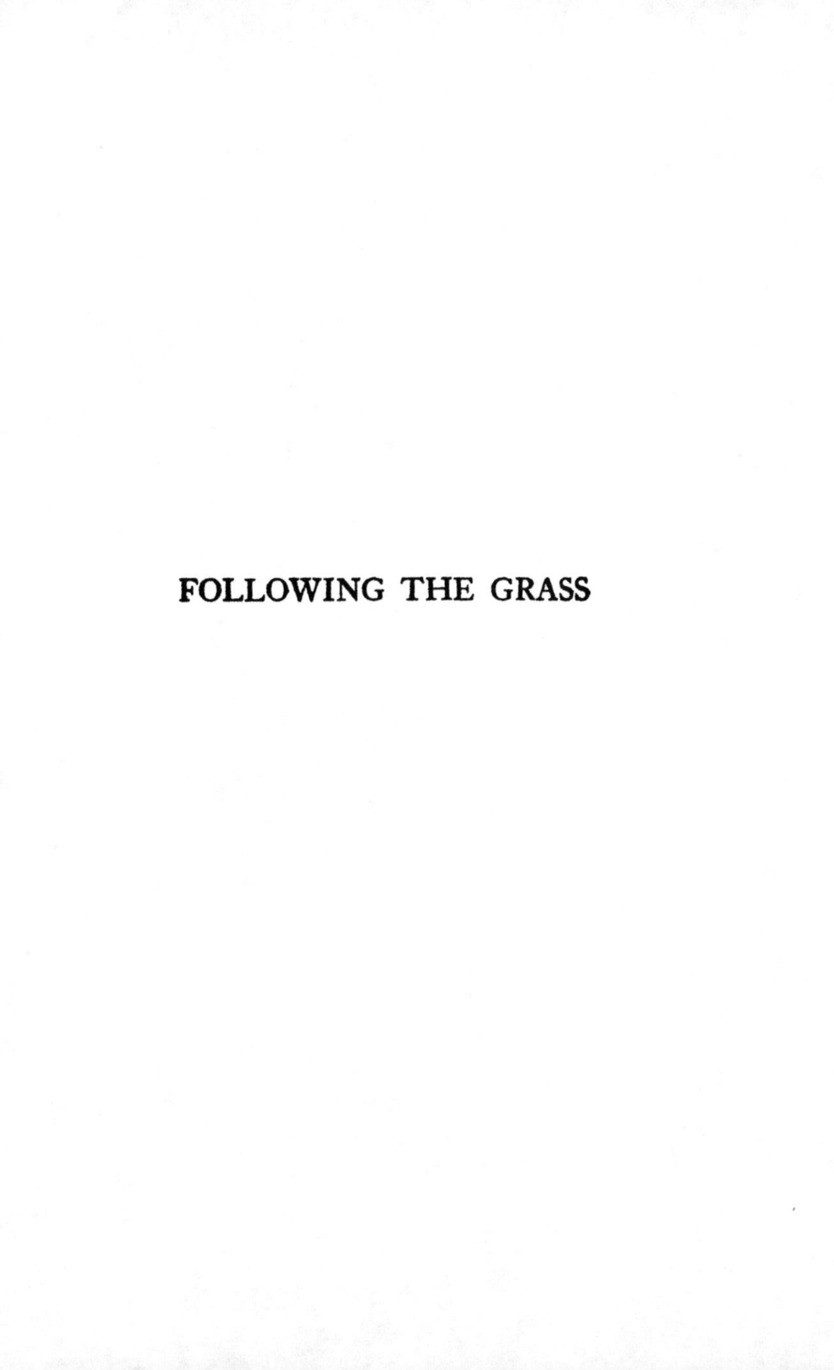

FOLLOWING THE GRASS

FOLLOWING THE GRASS

PROLOGUE.

I. THE COMING OF THE BASQUE.

High up among the Cantabrian foothills there is a *paramera*—a sealed valley. One enters and leaves it by a rocky trail that winds its way to the rim of the surrounding country by means of many tortuous grades. To the north, opposite the spot where the trail emerges from the valley, tower the grim, treeless, snow-capped Pyrenees—the great Basque barrier which armies and adventuring princes have assailed in vain.

It is a goodly country. There, for nine centuries or more, men have tilled the soil and herded their flocks; no one among them rich, and no one poor; bending the knee never to king or potentate. Seldom, indeed, have they even made a promise of allegiance to any ruler, and then only with such reservations as left them free men and the makers of their own laws and the keepers of their souls.

This day a man toiled up the trail which led to the outside world. He paused at the rim and let his pack sink to the ground. He was a mere boy, for all that his body was man-grown. His name was Angel Irosabal.

He was the eldest of ten sons, and yet, until to-day, he had never been out of the valley. This was equally true of his brothers. That Angel fared forth into strange lands to-day was only because he was turning his back forever on the valley of his fathers.

Since childhood he had worn the sleeveless sheepskin jerkin and leather breeches of the herder. He was in holiday garb to-day—rough homespun woven from the fleece of the sheep he himself had guarded, and fashioned to his figure by his mother's skilled hands.

Angel knew that as he proceeded through the valleys to come his attire alone would proclaim that some momentous event impended. And with good reason. Yet, surely, neither Angel nor his fellows could foresee that the business he was about was to change the course of history. Still, no less a thing was to come from it.

Take your map and place your finger upon the Bay of Biscay. You will see where the rocky coast of Biscay Province—old Vizcaya—turns back the surging tides. Nestling beside it is Alava, and beyond, to the north, hard-pressed by the Pyrenees and the Cantabrians, you will find Guipúscoa. It is a far-distant country, remote from the affairs of the world (or it was, then, in 1860), but during the previous year word of the new world had filtered into its upland valleys.

The New World—California! There was magic in its very name. Gold was hidden in its hillsides and streams; its wide valleys were rich, fertile beyond anything Guipúscoa knew. Rumor had it that those valleys only awaited the coming of man to be made to bloom as had the lowland gardens of Valencia.

It was a land where one rancho was larger than all of Guipúscoa—larger than all three of the Basque provinces put together! And men were their own masters there. They made their own laws!

Gray-haired Bonafacio, Angel's father, had whispered that tale to his sons. They had asked him many questions, for they knew that the soil of the *paramera* was almost exhausted. They had need of a new land; but the father had allowed a full year to pass before announcing his decision.

The time had come. One of them must go forth in search of a new country. When he had found it—be it California or South America—the rest would follow—all but the head and the youngest son of each family. This, so that their seed should not be lost to their native land.

They had heard him in silence, knowing that Angel, as the eldest, would be the one to go. Sober-faced, the boy had accepted his responsibility. A day of feasting had followed—several whole sheep had been roasted upon the spits; tankards had been filled with smoldering *chacoli*.

That was yesterday. This morning, Angel had taken up his pack and kissed his mother good-by. With his brothers to bear him company he had set off across the valley to where the trail began. There, in the gray dawn, a dry-eyed girl had met them. His brothers had turned back then, and Angel, left alone with the girl, had taken her in his arms and kissed her.

Both knew it was good-by; but there had been no tears. Angel would have held himself shamed had tears dimmed his eyes. Tears were for Catalans and Andalusians and other soft peoples of the plains. He was a Basque.

The girl was like him in this; not within the memory of man had a foreign taint crept into her blood. And so, although her heart was breaking, she had smiled bravely. It is the Basque way.

Even now, as Angel gazed down at the white-washed *caserio* of the Irosabals, his face was un-marred by emotion. He was an heroic figure as he stood there, tall, gaunt, with his hand shield-ing his eyes as he stared across the valley, his wind-tanned, copper-colored cheeks reflecting the rays of the westering sun.

Patiently his eyes swept the *paramera* until he located the landmarks of his boyhood. Old memories rushed to him and the minutes dragged by before he lowered his hand. From his pocket he took a blue magpie feather. When he had it firmly secured to a small rock he hurled it out into space, knowing that it would fall not far from where the trail began. It was the signal they had agreed on which should tell the girl that he had reached the top.

Picking up his pack, he turned his face toward Bilboa and the west. Spain was to know him no more. Later, for a brief two weeks, he loitered in Vera Cruz and Parral. In Mexico his Basque tongue was unknown, and so, by force of circum-stance, he had recourse to Spanish, a "second" language, which he spoke with greater elegance than Mexicans had been wont to hear.

Angel took no pride in this accomplishment.

Spanish had long been the language of business in the Basque Provinces, where, strangely, it had attained a degree of purity unknown outside of Seville. Hence, the boy's use of it was natural. In itself, it was a trivial matter. And yet, it was materially to affect his future life and the lives of those who were to follow in his footsteps.

El Camino Real—the king's highway—was still the great thoroughfare to California. In Parral Angel purchased a horse and joined a wagon-train bound for Los Angeles and Monterey. He went armed, as did his fellows, for even as late as 1861 the road led through a wild country.

America's attention was far from the Southwest. The great battles of the Civil War were being fought, and although the war touched the lives of those along the border, and volunteers for both sides were not wanting, it was with the problems which the war brought, rather than with the war itself, that the frontier was concerned. Their old enemies, the Apaches and the Teguas, had sensed the relaxing of the restraining hand to which they had submitted. If history does not record those turbulent days in the Southwest it is only because they were concurrent with events of far greater importance east of the Mississippi.

Angel was essentially a fighting-man. The days that followed were to his liking. As the wagon-train moved north tales of the great battles came with increasing frequency. Had the boy been free to do as he pleased he surely would have turned his back on California. But the war was not for him.

Soon after the train turned west its troubles began. More than once Angel's nostrils dilated to the acrid smell of gunpowder. A month later, tired and saddle-worn, he crossed into California. There, the war divided attention with the Comstock and Yuba River. Gold was on everyone's tongue. California was not only the greatest country in the world: it was the richest. Just wait until the war was won!

Now the boy's way led ever northward; through the San Joaquin valley, past the Merced, the Tuolumne, the Sacramento. He was in a sheepman's paradise. Even the Pyrenees could not match the Sierra Nevada.

The basin narrowed as he left Sacramento behind him. He took to the hills and explored upland valleys that dwarfed the *paramera* of his childhood. No longer did great flocks of short-wooled merinos greet his eye. Here was only talk of gold, of the fortunes being taken out of the Feather and the Yuba.

Angel knew he had found the place he sought. The soil was light, sandy—the very finest in the world for sheep. Bunch-grass, wild clover and a variety of salt bush were abundant. Timber was to hand, also. Nothing was wanting. Land was cheap.

The very bigness of the country was in its favor. In three days' journey he had not seen a fence. Best of all, this land was not unlike his homeland. Therefore, from old Nevada City he dispatched word to Guipúscoa.

The residents of Nevada City were not of a discerning mind. To them, Angel was just another Mexican. His features, hair, the color of his skin and his stature should have marked a difference in their eyes, but they failed of it; and largely because Irosabal had a Spanish ring to it, and because the boy spoke Spanish. Later, when out of loneliness and the desire for speech, he consorted with Mexicans, the term "greaser" was applied to him without question.

At the time, the term of contempt meant nothing to Angel. He had not a dozen words of English at his command. Later, though, it was to make a difference. And the tragedy of it! Had he come to California knowing not a word of Spanish, he would have been received as was his due—the first of a distinct, proud, industrious and thrifty race. Instead of which he dowered himself and his brothers with the contempt reserved by Americans for the shiftless, lazy, gambling Mexican peon.

But no matter. Winter was at hand. It proved to be a mild one. Angel went back to the hills and built a cabin. Very little snow fell in the mountains that year. No one appeared to notice the fact, least of all the boy busy with his plans for the coming of his people. Spring came early. In April, he went to Sacramento to meet his brothers.

The newspapers of that day make bare mention of their coming; and yet, there were more than forty in the party—men, women, children. Most of them were related to Angel. The girl to whom he had tossed the blue magpie feather was among them.

Her coming was a surprise arranged by Angel's father. They were married the following day. By the end of the week the party had been provisioned and properly outfitted. Lambing-time was nearly over; the season for buying and selling breeders would follow immediately. Before it began, Angel's party had to be housed. Therefore, he led the way to the valley south of Nevada City without further delay.

There began then such a job of pioneering as

America has seldom witnessed. The year was to be long remembered in California. What snow there was in the mountains went off rapidly. The streams rose over night. Sacramento was devastated.

Close on the heels of the flood began the severest drouth in California's history. By mid-summer, cattle and sheep were starving. Horses were slaughtered in great numbers in order to save range for the cattle.

Conditions grew steadily worse. Not once during the long hot months did rain fall in the Sacramento Basin. To the north and east, where the foot-hills were timbered, the bunch-grass and dwarf sage survived.

Angel's people profited by this. They were able to buy sheep at their own price. No wonder, then, that before winter came again they were cordially hated by the less fortunate sheepmen of the Basin. And now, for the second year in succession, were the mountains free of snow. The fact was noted this time. It was an ominous sign: Spring but proved it—the drouth was unbroken; even in the hills, the sage, hardiest of plants, withered and died.

II. FOLLOWING THE GRASS.

THERE was nothing for Angel and his people to do but move. But to where? No one came forward to offer them range or help them in their extremity. They were a people apart.

But they knew how to meet misfortune with a brave face. The houses which they had built, the corrals, the crops which they had planted—these and all of the fruits of a year of hard, unremitting, back-breaking toil were lost to them if they moved. Undaunted, they chose to drive their flocks to some new country where they could begin again, to follow the grass as sheepmen ever have done.

Their courage brought them one reward—a new and distinct term of contempt. They were no longer "greasers"; they were "boscos"—a strange corruption of the Spanish *Basque.* "Greasers" quit; these "boscos" were fighters, and accordingly, they were to be watched. There were too many foreigners in California, anyhow!

The Central Pacific was being built. Already

the railhead was beyond the Sierra Nevada. Along this route, then, did Angel and his followers go. Those who had horses rode, the others walked, driving their herds before them. In the rear thundered their wagons. California was glad to be rid of them. But it was California's loss.

For nearly a century the way of the pioneer had led westward. Here, then, was the first trek eastward. It made history, for it brought to Nevada its greatest factional fight—the war of the cowboy and the herder. The big cattle-outfits were well established in the valleys north of the Humboldt.

Range was free, but there was no room for sheep. There had been trouble enough already over sheep. Arizona had had a taste of it. Sheep were a Mexican business anyhow.

Nevada was a new state and things were lax, but even if the politicians down in the old Washoe country had no concern with anything that did not affect mining and Virginia City, folks north of the Humboldt could look after themselves. So along the river, from Dufrayne's mill to Fort Halleck, the warning went up—"Sheepmen Stay Out!"

The cowmen did not lack arguments for the stand they took. Sheep huddle closely while grazing. They have an upper and lower set of teeth: so they virtually crop grass and herbage to the very roots, and what they do not eat their knife-like hoofs destroy.

With free-range, it was not to be supposed that herders would keep their flocks moving. At that time, no one gave a thought to the future. The universal intention was to rip out a fortune in a hurry.

If cattle did not destroy the range it was because of the habits with which nature had endowed them, not because of the care or foresight of the men who owned them. Equal carelessness with sheep meant the ruining of the range; for if they grazed time and again over the same land, nothing could survive on it, not even the sheep themselves.

And this was the country to which Angel, as a last resort, led his people! So far, they had followed the railroad, but the construction gangs had only reached the Truckee; so at the river they took the trail to Fort McDermitt. In a general way, their objective was the Owyhee Basin, or, denied that, the valleys of the Tuscarora Range to the south of the Basin.

Before them stretched an arid, semi-desert country. There were no towns. White men were few. In a sense, it was Indian country, for although the Piute was, to all intent, peaceful, he had not forgotten what he and his brothers had done to the white man at Pyramid Lake.

Observe this immigration, then, for what it was—a journey of privation, danger and hardship beneath a scorching sun, and undertaken without previous knowledge of the country through which they were to pass. At the river-crossings, quicksands awaited them; when they left the river their children were to cry and their own tongues grow thick for want of water.

They knew nothing of the desert. They were even less fitted, by experience, for their task than the men and women who had followed Brigham Young across the plains. And at their journey's end, if they won through, was what? Organized hostility, hatred and contempt!

The picture is well-nigh hopeless. Add to it that they were to stop not less than three times to bury their dead beside the trail; that four of their women were to know the anguish and travail of childbirth. Is there aught of misery that was not theirs?

And yet they triumphed. Eventually, in July it was, they crossed the Humboldt for the last time. They were just south of Winnemucca Mountain at about the spot where the town of Winnemucca now stands.

Here the Little Humboldt joins the big river.

Due to some miraculous urge of fortune, they chose to follow the smaller stream. It was a happy choice, for surely they never would have been suffered to cross the Tuscaroras.

Almost immediately the country began to change. Small, fertile valleys opened before them. The grass grew green in the creek bottoms; in the distance low, friendly, grayish-green hills, fringed with stunted cedars, arose. Water was always to hand; the creeks were heading in those hills ahead—Willow Creek, Rebel Creek, Martin Creek and a score of small streams as yet unnamed.

Martin Creek was the largest. Soon they came to the spot where it flows into the Little Humboldt. The river bore away to the northeast; the creek's course lay to the north, its promise unmistakable. It was not to be denied!

Angel's party turned to the north. Unknowingly, they were entering the garden spot of northern Nevada—Paradise Valley, so named, ten years before, by a cavalry lieutenant who left his bones to whiten there.

Angel, his five days' old daughter in his arms, was the first of his party across the Martin. He was not aware of a tall, sinewy, sullen-faced man and a boy, a lad of nine, who sat in their saddles upon the opposite bank staring at them as they forced the sheep across the shallow ford.

The man and boy were father and son. A trader had opened a store on Cottonwood Creek (destined to become the town of Paradise), and they had been on their way there when they caught sight of the Basque caravan. Open hostility had flashed in the man's eyes. He was a cowman, a Kentuckian named David Gault. Sheep were as little to his liking as they were to the big outfits in the Basin.

The boy, Joseph, shared his father's anger. In silence, they waited for the strangers to draw near.

"Hit's greasers, all right," the boy said at last, his mouth hard. "Reckon they air comin' to stay!"

The man shook his head. "Ain't no room fer sheep ner greasers in this yere country, Joseph. We fit the Injuns fer hit; hit's ourn. Ain't no furriners goin' ter take hit from us. Let 'em come with their sheep—they won't stay long!"

Gault was mistaken. Not only were the Basques to cling tenaciously to Paradise Valley, they were to prosper there, raise their families, draw reinforcements from distant valleys in the Pyrenees and, in the end, become American citizens. And this despite the fact that they were to be reviled, scorned, cheated and warred on for twenty years. Later, the term "greaser" was to be unheard; throughout Nevada and Idaho they were to be just "boscos," and the word was to be uttered with such bitterness as the Mexican had never drawn.

Early in those twenty years the Central Pacific was to be completed. Prosperity was to follow; towns were to be built—Winnemucca, Golconda, Tuscarora. New settlers were to come, bringing banks, schools and churches.

Among the newcomers there were to be impartial men, but even these were to regard the Basques as a sullen, clannish, not-understandable race. They were to trust them at their banks; for no man could say but what they were honest, prompt in the paying of their debts; but it was only the banker who was to accept the Basque as a proud, thrifty, hard-working man, and therefore a good risk.

And the Basques were to repay their enemies in their own coin. They were, indeed, to become a sullen people, but they had ever been lovers of solitude, dependent on their family life for social pleasures. So, driven in on themselves, they were to become clannish to a degree the Basque had never known in his own land. They knew how to hate and bear a grudge, and, Indian-like, they would not forget.

Twenty years were to bring Basque saloons, inns, stores and forwarding-agents to Winnemucca and Golconda. Paradise was to become a Basque town. What a Basque wanted, he bought from a Basque. Let these *gringos* keep to themselves! They wanted nothing of them. If sheep were killed, cattle could be killed, too; and it often happened that they were.

Angel Irosabal was to foster this spirit. He was to become rich; the father of many children, although none was to take the place of the little Margarida, who had been born in a covered wagon. To those of the rising generation to whom he was not bound by blood, he became *padrino* (godfather), a tie as binding as the blood strain.

His *ahijados* were to be counted by the score. And between himself and the fathers of these children was to exist a bond known only to *compadres*. It was to make him supreme among the Basques.

He was to be the fount of wisdom. For ten years, and for twice ten years, they were to follow him, and he was to rule not only wisely, but well, instilling pride of race in the young—preaching and convincing them of the enormity of their sin should they take to husband or wife one of an alien race. And yet, in the richest years of his life he was to hold himself shamed, betrayed; and the dimpling, black-eyed babe whom he held in his arms to-day, was to be the cause of it.

No hint of that distant shadow rested upon Angel as he pulled his horse to a stop beside the cattleman and his son. A pleasant word was on his tongue as he bowed with Old World courtesy to Gault.

Gault's answer was a sneering grunt: "I don't know where yo're from, stranger, and hit don't matter, nohow; but I'm a-tellin' ye yuh've toted yore stuff a long ways fer nuthin'. Yo're a-goin' back—way back! This is white folks' country. Ain't no sheepmen a-comin' in yere! Don't yuh bother 'bout unloadin' them waggins. I'm tellin' yuh—git 'em turned about by ter-morrow! Yuh can't stay here!"

Gault was not bluffing; and if time was to prove him mistaken, it was only to be after years of violence and bloodshed. So it was with an angry clanking of spur-chains that he wheeled his horse and galloped away, the boy at his heels.

Half an hour later they pulled their horses to a walk. Gault glanced at his son.

"Yore face is white, Joseph," he drawled.

"The trouble yore mammy saw in her cup is a-comin'. Ye ain't skeered, be yuh?"

"I ain't skeered a nuthin'," the lad answered bravely. "I reckon I kin shoot straight."

"Well, hit'll git to shootin', if they try ter stay. Yore mammy an' me ain't a-goin' ter move again; we're too old. Other folks round hyar is like us. Ain't no one a-goin' ter take away what's ourn by right."

"But the man had a baby in his arms. What's a-goin' ter become of hit if thar's shootin'?"

"Humph! Don't ye go worryin' 'bout no greaser kid, Joseph. Ain't nuthin' could mean less ter yuh."

And now score one for Fate! David Gault and Angel Irosabal were to be laid low by the same blow; for no less a thing was to occur than that the son of one was to woo and win the daughter of the other; and defying prejudice, ostracism and religious as well as racial barriers, they were to wed—the boy to be held no better than a squaw-man by his people, and the girl an outcast by her race.

But their love for each other was to sustain them. And it is with the second Joseph, the fruit of their marriage, that this story is chiefly concerned.

CHAPTER I.

THE STORM.

THE days of that August had been sunless. At rare intervals, and then for only an hour or two, would the leaden skies part for a reassuring glimpse of the blue heavens beyond. The air was heavy with silence, and although the weather was warm, that stillness which hung over mesa and valley was not unlike the hush which ushers in the violent storms of winter.

The woman in the herder's cabin, far up the side of Buckskin Mountain, busy with her bread-making, paused to glance down at the wide valley which stretched away from the base of the mountain to the Timbered Buttes far to the west. Even at the distance from which she observed it, it took definite shape; the fringes of green willows and buckthorn clearly defining the course Martin Creek took as it zigzagged across the valley. Likewise, the never-failing willows marked where the smaller streams cut through to the Martin.

Moving smudges of color she recognized for

cattle. The same sense told her that they were not grazing; they were moving too rapidly. Subconsciously, she wondered if they, too, had been made uneasy by this stillness which hung so heavily in the air. She was a Basque, and therefore superstitious enough to believe that it portended some evil.

And yet, the face, which she pressed to the window to-day seemed marked with something deeper than mere transient apprehension. It was a singularly beautiful face—serious, delicate—the skin a pale olive tint. Her hair was as black as night, and her eyes blacker than any night. But although her eyes—lonely, wistful—arrested the attention, it was her mouth—patient, contented— hinting of suffering and the conquering of suffering—that was unforgettable.

There were no other cabins on Buckskin. Often for weeks on end no one passed the door. The few who did were prospectors or Indians. They never tarried, and so there was no one to carry the tale of that face so often pressed to the window.

On clear days, the woman — she was only twenty-five — could see the town of Paradise. There were no other settlements within forty miles. What supplies they needed, her husband either carried or hauled from there.

If her eyes sought to pierce the haze that hung over the valley to-day for a glimpse of Paradise, it was only because her husband was there, or by now returning from there. Oftenest, her eyes sought the white-washed house and ranch buildings to the north and east of the little town which even distance could not rob of an air of prosperity. Angel Irosabal, the headman of the Basques, lived there.

She was that mighty man's daughter!—and yet, for eight full years she had not entered there, nor in all that time—through sickness, the birth of her son—had one of her own blood exchanged a word with her. There were brothers and sisters of hers in that big house, a mother, too; but if they wondered about her, or hoped that the stern father would relent, Margarida Gault, the herder's wife, had no sign of it.

Eight years is a long time for a father to bear a grudge; it is an equally long time to keep hope of forgiveness alive. Joe Gault's wife had come to believe that the years would never be so many that her father would open his arms to her.

Always she told her husband it didn't matter; that she no longer cared. Often she whispered as much to herself; but on the days when Gault went to town, or when he was away on the mountain, some mad impulse drove her to the window. She believed it to be only habit, and she tried to fight it; but when once the desire had planted itself in her brain, torturing hours of restlessness always followed, and often defeated her.

At the window, she found peace, of a sort; and she never left it without breathing a prayer that God might soften her father's heart; for surely in His eyes no sin was hers. She had but married the man she loved.

That he was of another religion, and of a breed of men who had persecuted her people, was her only transgression. That thought sustained her. . . . She was not a penitent.

If her husband never mentioned her father's name, it was not because he failed to read the message in her eyes. He understood. And much of the business which took him over the mountain was only invented so that the bitterness in his heart could be voiced unheard by her.

There were other Gaults in the valley, kinsmen of his—the old Cross-K outfit—but he never mentioned them. In fact he had long since forgotten them; but he had never been able to forget the man who had put that hungry look in his wife's eyes.

Daily, in countless ways, he tried to make up for what marrying him had cost her, and he came as near to succeeding as love, and patience, and unfailing kindness can come. But some few there were who pitied Margarida Gault. They wondered how she withstood the loneliness of that little cabin perched high upon the mountainside.

Gault, so they said, was a cowman; how could he expect to have luck with sheep—and on Buckskin Mountain of all places! If the cattle-outfits and the big sheepmen kept their hands off Buckskin it was because the range was so poor that even the jack-rabbits refused it.

And yet for all their talk, Gault's sheep grew fat. There was timber-clover in those little parks of stunted cedars and junipers on the mountaintop. Valley men said it was bad for sheep and cattle; it bloated them and they often died. But Gault found that his sheep thrived on it if they cropped it for only two or three days at a time.

So if his industry fell short of making him a prosperous man, it at least provided the essential things of life, and that pitying few in Paradise Valley would have been surprised had they known that the snug wee cabin on Buckskin often echoed to happy laughter. It was the abiding place of love, the shrine of an infant god who held the hearts of Joseph and Margarida Gault in his pudgy little hands.

He was called Joseph, too—a manly lad of seven, with his father's reddish-brown hair and his Basque mother's finely chiseled features. He was old for his years, and already self-reliant; in his eyes was a wisdom as of the aged. It was a baffling look. To his parents it seemed as if he were reading their souls, and not their lips.

Margarida had first noticed it one day as she turned from the window her eyes filled with tears. She had smiled and kissed him, but his expression had not changed. It seemed that he saw through her pretense and understood the grief which ate at her heart. It had left her with an uncanny feeling, and she was careful to see that the child's questioning eyes never found tears in her own again.

He had been in the kitchen with her to-day, but the angry cawing of a flock of crows had drawn him outside. She had heard him calling to them as they circled about the cabin scolding the laggard leader of the flock. Joseph often talked to the crows and the magpies.

This was disquieting to Margarida; for it brought home so poignantly his loneliness. Even Indian boys played and romped with other children. No wonder then, that Joseph turned to the wild for companionship. He was only answering a primitive instinct which had come down to him through many generations of roving fathers.

It was, however, in a self-accusing frame of

mind that Margarida went on with her work. The afternoon was well along, and by the time she had finished her baking it was dark in the kitchen. She had not known it was so late. A glance at the clock, however, showed that twilight should still be an hour away. Alarmed, she ran to the door and called:

"Joseph! Jo-o-seph!"

The air had grown so cool that she shivered as she stood in the doorway waiting for the boy's answer. Uneasy, she called again, and when her second call went unanswered, she rolled up her apron and started off toward the coulee where the dogs were holding the herd for the night.

She stopped, when she had gone a hundred yards from the cabin, and called again. As she waited, the stillness, which had settled heavier than ever over the mountain, seemed to clutch at her. Not a leaf was stirring, and although it was the time of evening when the whippoorwills sail over the sage-brush, there was not a wing in the air, nor could she catch sound of their plaintive, mocking call. She crossed herself nervously, and turned an anxious eye toward the road which led up from the valley, wishing that her husband was home, but knowing that he would not come for another hour at least.

Joseph had not answered, so she picked up her

skirts, and half ran to the coulee. The shadows were deepening, but she could see the flock standing uneasily, apparently loath to bed down for the night. The dogs were running back and forth, grumbling to themselves, as if by this show of authority they hoped to make the flock lie down. They paused only for a second on catching sight of Margarida, for they sensed even better than the sheep that something was amiss. Their mistress's excitement was quickly communicated to them, too, and they barked sharply.

Margarida had expected to find Joseph with the dogs, but a hurried glance told her that they were alone. Her throat went dry with fear as she realized the truth. What could have happened to him? Her hands shook as she raised them to her mouth. *"Jovencito!"* she cried. "Where are you? Answer me!"

She stopped suddenly as she caught sight of the milling sheep in the center of the flock. They were kicking up a great dust. A moment later, from out the dust-cloud, rode Joseph, astraddle a snorting ram!

Margarida could only hold her breath. She was afraid to call to him, for if the ram bucked him off before he got to the edge of the flock, the sheep would be panic-stricken immediately.

Once upon the ground, the child would be ground to death by their sharp hoofs.

What had tempted him to do this thing? Was he without any sense of fear? She knew it was remarkable that the animal permitted Joseph to ride him at all. This particular ram had been running wild on the range all summer, and he was possessed of a fiendish temper and a dangerous sense of dignity.

And yet as she watched, Joseph caught sight of her, and, although he called and waved his hands, the ram did not buck. In five minutes, he had ridden clear of the flock. The dogs tried to turn the ram, but Joseph urged him on, and not until he was within a few feet of his mother did the boy slip to the ground. The animal waited to have his ears scratched and then, with lowered head, he dashed back into the flock.

Margarida ran to the child and caught him up. "Joseph!" she murmured, "you frightened me so. I've been calling and calling for you, *muchachito.* What if you had fallen?"

"Grandpa wouldn't throw me, mother," the child answered stoutly.

"Grandpa—you call him Grandpa?" Margarida exclaimed, aghast.

"Well, he looks mean like grandpas look," Joseph declared naïvely.

"Hush—hush—Joseph!" Margarida crooned as she pressed her cheek to his. *"Cállate, jovencito.* Maybe to-morrow we can find a better name for the ram. But we must go, it is night. Let me have your hand, *niño!"*

Even though they hurried along, it was black night before they reached the little draw in which the cabin sat. A thin, piercing scream—far-off and ever rising—struck their ears. With each step they took, it grew. Margarida clutched Joseph's hand. The air about them seemed to tremble.

"Run, Joseph!" Margarida warned. But the next moment the full fury of the wind struck them and knocked them down. Suddenly the air was filled with whirling sand. Great clouds of it were scooped out of the mountain and hurled at them. It cut the eyes and scourged the cheeks. Choking and half blinded, Margarida turned her back to the wind, and with Joseph in her arms staggered to her feet. The cabin was nearly a hundred yards away, and Joseph was heavy for her, but with strength she had little suspected she possessed she swung him up and went on. In spite of her efforts she sank to her knees again and again.

With every passing second the storm grew in violence. The wind was ripping out sage-brush and greasewood and hurling it into the air. Once, a piece of buckthorn struck her and drew blood. Mountain and valley were being swept clean of debris. Branches and limbs of dead willows and mahogany tress, and all the litter of the range, were in that wild maelstrom.

No cry escaped the boy's lips and, although his mouth and eyes were closed tightly, the expression on his face was not one of fear. Even with his mother's body to shield him from the screaming storm, the razor-edged sand seared his little face. When she fell, he snuggled to her and waited patiently for her to rise and go on again. Later—it seemed a long time—he heard her kick open the cabin door.

Once inside, Margarida let Joseph slip to the floor. The gale was rocking the cabin, the windows were rattling and the door banging back and forth as if the storm was intent on ripping it from its fastenings.

With an angry cry, Margarida hurled her body against it and forced it shut. Through every crack and cranny the fine sand was sifting in. It grated beneath her feet as she ran to the kitchen for a lamp. The light flickered fitfully as she placed it upon the table; and as she went about poking bits of rags into the crevices it cast weird shadows of herself upon the walls and ceiling.

Joseph was thrilled rather than alarmed. He hurried about believing he was helping his mother; but Margarida soon found that it was impossible to keep the sand from coming in, and as she gave up trying, Joseph voiced the very question that was stabbing at her heart:

"Where is daddy, mother?"

"Under shelter, I hope, Joseph. He must have left the valley before the storm broke. He'd know it was coming. If he made the box cañon this side of the Circle-Z fence, he's safe. No horse could keep a trail on such a night. I'm only afraid that he'll be worried about us, and try to get here before the storm is over.

"Your father is a good man, Joseph. You ask God to take care of him. We wouldn't know what to do without him. *Virgen santísima!*" she entreated as she sank to her knees, "don't let him risk that trail to-night." She crossed herself and waited for Joseph to do the same, but the boy was staring off into space. He did not arise when Margarida got to her feet. He was muttering something, and listening, she heard him say:

"Oh, God, take good care of my daddy. My mother needs him, 'cause I ain't old enough to be a man yet. You tell him we're all right, and not to be scared. But if he's going to come, You tell his horse where to go. Old Pepper is smart; he'll understand what You tell him."

Without further sign the boy got to his feet. His mother looked at him speechlessly. "You don't cross yourself, Joseph?" she asked at last.

"I do when I pray, mother; but I don't like to pray. I was just talking to God then. I often talk to Him when I'm on the mountain."

Just why this simple statement should bring a mist to her eyes, Margarida did not know, but her voice trembled as she asked:

"And what does He say to you, my little son?"

"He tells me how to make friends with things. Guess there ain't nuthin' on the mountain that's afraid of me."

The child's simple honesty made him a pathetic figure. Unconsciously he but emphasized his loneliness. Margarida shook her head as she set about getting supper. Joseph's talk frightened her, and she resolved that at any cost she would see that he went to the valley in the fall.

The child was hungry, and he ate what his mother placed before him. The whining wind and the sound of the sand beating against the window panes filled the room as they sat at the table. Margarida ate but little. By the time they had finished, it was Joseph's bedtime.

An hour later, the dishes washed, and the sand

swept up again, Margarida ventured to open the door, hoping to find some sign of the storm's passing; but the night was wilder than ever. It was nine o'clock, and as the minutes droned by and her husband did not come, she took courage; for if he had not sought shelter he would have been there by now—or else he never would come!

And while she waited for him, two men—Race Eagan and Tiny Mears—squatted beside their sage-brush fire far under the protecting wall of the box cañon north of the Circle-Z fence. This fence was a line fence and, although a drift fence had been built below it, it never sufficed, in bad weather, to hold the herd.

Farther west, this line fence became the barrier for the big sheep-outfits. In fact, this Piute Meadows fence, as it was called, had been the scene of two bloody battles and numerous minor affrays. Whenever the Circle-Z was seriously annoyed the trouble was along this line.

Race and Tiny had been "riding" the fence. The storm had caught them out in the open. They had fought it for an hour before dashing to cover. They were fairly out of the gale beneath the overhanging wall, but their horses stood with heads lowered, their manes and forelocks flattened out before them in the wind.

"No use our sittin' here," Tiny grumbled.

"Might as well turn in. This zephyr is a-goin' to last all night."

"Yeh, and there'll be Circle-B steers all over hell to-morrow," Egan agreed.

"Ain't our fault. I'm a-goin' to sleep."

Tiny's preparation for bed was limited to the unrolling of his blanket and the removal of boots and chaps. He was about to lie down when Race saw him stiffen.

"What's the matter, Tiny?" Egan asked banteringly. "The wind scare you so to-night?"

"Didn't yuh hear it?" Tiny whispered.

"What?"

"A shot! I heard it plain—off there to the west. The wind would carry the sound a long ways to-night."

"Yeh, and all this stuff that's flyin' around in the air would kill it in a short ways. Ain't nobody out in this storm. Kit's over west, but that cagy boy ain't nestin' in a fence corner. He's somewhere where it's warm and—"

Race felt Tiny's fingers close upon his ankle, and he stopped short. Their faces grim, they stared at each other.

"D'yuh hear it then?" Tiny asked anxiously.

Race nodded. "Sure did!" he muttered. "Reckon it wa'n't far off, either. Pull on your boots, Tiny. We got to go."

CHAPTER II.

THE STAMPEDE.

JOE GAULT could read the weather as can only a man born and bred on the range. When he rode out of Paradise at five o'clock in the afternoon of that day, he knew the storm would strike in a few hours. He spurred his horse to a sharp hand-canter as he turned eastward. Pepper's free-swinging stride made light of the long, desert miles, but the storm came on with speed that mocked the animal's best. Gault's eyes swept the sky.

"Hit's shore a-goin' to come soon," he muttered aloud, "an' hit's a-goin to be a fence twister, too. Mought a-known hit would come to-night. Reckon we'll just about make the fence by the time she strikes."

He had usually allowed himself four hours for the journey from Paradise to the cabin. At the speed at which he rode to-night he would lessen that by at least a full hour, but as the minutes passed he realized that even such a saving would not see him home in time. He had not yet reached the Circle-Z fence when the darkness which had settled so early upon the mountain, cloaked the valley. Within half an hour man and horse caught the first sound of that wild, high-pitched humming which was rushing toward them from the west.

The box cañon north of the fence was still some miles away, but it was not of it that Gault thought as he pulled his hat low over his eyes and tied his neckerchief over his mouth and nose. He had been glancing up the mountain for the light which Margarida always burned for him. He could not locate it to-night. It worried him, even though he told himself that the night was so heavy a light could not be seen so far.

He knew that nothing could have happened to Margarida or Joseph, but the very fact that he could not see their light made him more anxious than ever to be home. He knew his sheep would fret until the storm was upon them, but the dogs would hold the flock. When the sand began to fill the air, it would be hard to drive the sheep from the coulee, for they were sheltered from the wind, there.

The storm struck then with a mad rush and abruptly terminated Gault's chain of thought. Pepper snorted and lowered his head, but he went on, his eyes half closed, preferring anything to turning about and facing the blinding sand. It was impossible to see ahead for more than ten feet, so Gault kept his horse to the fence. In this fashion they went on for an hour.

Pepper stumbled as he slid down into a little arroyo. He nickered pitifully as he straightened up. Gault reached out his hands and covered the animal's eyes. As if grateful for the kindness, the horse broke into a canter.

Later, they dropped into a dry-wash. For a brief minute they were out of the full sweep of the wind. Gault recognized the place and knew that they had only two miles to go before reaching the draw where they were to turn off on the trail which led up the mountain. For some time, sub-consciously, he had been calculating the chance of being able to climb Buckskin.

Pepper knew the trail well enough, but in places it was steep and dangerous, a misstep in the dark would plunge them to death. But this weighing of difficulties amounted to less than nothing, for Gault knew that he would make the attempt.

Not long after they came out of the wash he fancied he heard the barking of dogs. He listened carefully, but he did not catch the sound again. As far as he knew, his own dogs were the only ones within miles. If they were with the flock in the coulee the wind was against his hearing them; still, he would have sworn he had heard the baying of dogs, and directly ahead of him, too. It made him uneasy, and he urged his horse on. He had not gone more than a hundred yards before a shot, deep and muffled, boomed in his ears.

The horse heard it, too, and tossed up his head. Gault stopped him in his tracks and listened intently. It seemed that the noise of the storm would drown the sound of a shot, unless it were near. Gault admitted that he might have been mistaken about having heard dogs barking—a coyote would have accounted for it—but there was no mistaking that shot.

And then, as he waited, it came again—the deep-toned bark of a high-powered gun! Gault thought he caught a flash of spurting flame almost simultaneously with the second shot. The Circle-Z fence turned south here, and it was where it came back to the north, less than a quarter of a mile away, that he believed the streak of flame had stabbed the darkness. He had his gun in his hand by now and, in spite of the storm, Pepper dashed ahead as Gault raked him with the spurs.

Gault swung himself to the ground as he came abreast the corner of the fence, and with the reins in his hands he stumbled toward it, dragging Pepper after him. A gasp of astonishment was rung from him as he saw that the fence was down. Hand over hand he went along it until he came to the place where it had been cut. He ran his fingers over the sharp ends of the wire. "God!" he muttered. "Ain't no sheep nor cattle done hit. That's nippers!"

Pepper almost pulled the rein out of Gault's hand as the herder bent again to examine the fence. When the horse came down he stood stiff legged, snorting with fear. Gault raised his voice to speak to the horse when a confusion of sounds which rose above the bellowing of the storm struck him. The next instant the barking of dogs and the mad bleating and baaing of sheep reached his ears.

"God A'mighty!" he cried out, and his voice shook, "how am I a-goin' turn 'em?"

He was in his saddle already and dashing toward the oncoming flock. Instinctively he sensed that they were his own sheep. From the direction from which they came there could be no doubt of it. . . . There were no sheep but his on Buckskin!

But what had happened? It wasn't sheep nature to fight dogs and storm. If the flock had started to drift it would have gone the other way. But the answer was not far to seek. Gault shook his head grimly; he knew!

It was not coincidence that found the Circle-Z fence down in the flock's very path. Things didn't happen that way on the range. Whoever had cut the wire had known that the sheep were being stampeded. Once through the fence, the flock certainly would turn to the east. There the deep cañon of the North Fork of the Little Humboldt cut across the Circle-Z country.

Gault's sheep would not be the first ones that had been swept over the rim-rocks to their death. If they missed that fate, they still would be trespassing on Circle-Z range, and they would be put off—and the manner of their ejection would not be pretty to see. The fence-cutting would have to be explained, too. The evidence was only circumstantial, but it was damning; range law had convicted men on less.

Gault knew that the Circle-Z waddies rode this fence every night. The shooting which he had heard had undoubtedly occurred when one of them had found the wire cut. Storm or no storm, they would be back before long. Trouble would ride with them.

Gault felt trapped. Who had done this thing to him? Not the Circle-Z; Thad Taylor was no friend of his, but this game was a cut beneath anything the old cattleman would lend himself to. Besides, he had nothing that Taylor wanted.

This blow had been aimed by some one who hoped to drive him out. It had been tried before, in other ways; but the Basque *gente* had not succeeded with the organized discouragement which they had doled out so adroitly. In back of this stampede was hatred, revenge! Gault recognized it for what it was. It aroused his fighting-blood.

He had always beaten them. The thought stiffened his lip, and wheeling his horse, he swung the animal broadside to the sheep which were swarming against him. Rising in his saddle he bellowed to the dogs. They recognized him and ran toward him. As they came on Gault fanned his gun. The sheep began to mill as the leaders shied back from the barking gun and the flashing teeth of the dogs.

Gault forced his horse into the flock as he saw the leaders checked. For an instant, the billowing sea of wool appeared to rock back and forth. Gault saw that the storm aided him, for as the flock lost momentum the sheep turned their heads away from the biting sand.

It was the advantage he hoped to gain, and he crowded them back step by step. His dogs, almost as wise as he in the ways of sheep, followed his lead. Gault began bawling in a sing-song tone:

"Coo-sheep!   C' sh'p!   Coo-o-o- — sheep!
Co—she', coo—she', coo-o—sheep!"

The next second or two would bring the decision. The sheep in the center of the flock were wavering already. If they got away now, it would be caused by the sheep in the rear pouring around the edge of the flock. Gault kept on calling, but he held his hands to his eyes and tried to see what was happening to the left and right of him.

He cursed as he saw an old ram break free. His gun leaped out and he pulled, but the pistol was empty. He was about to hurl it at the ram when one of the dogs leaped into the air and knocked the animal end over end. In less than a minute the flock was flowing up the mountain!

One of the dogs hung back and howled. Gault rode over to him, expecting to find a sheep with a broken leg. Even from his saddle he saw that there was something on the ground. He loaded his gun before he got down, intending to shoot the animal if it were badly hurt; but as he got to his knees and reached out to turn it over, his blood turned cold. The thing before him, half buried in the drifting sand, was the body of a man!

It was still warm. Gault struck a light four or five times before he managed to get a glimpse of the man's face.

"Kit Dorr!" he gasped as he recognized him. Gault's eyes bulged from their sockets as he caught another look at the man before his match flared out. "Dead—! He's shore dead!" he muttered. "God A'mighty, this is a-goin' to be terrible bad for me, Kit! Hit shore is!"

Gault got to his feet and stood looking down at the dead man, his head shaking wearily.

"They shore got me this time," he drawled. "Folks all know we had words; and the wire cut; my sheep stampedin' around, and one or two got through the fence, like as not—God A'mighty! Ain't no man a-goin' to believe I didn't kill you, Kit; ain't but one or two even a-goin' to try to believe hit. Reckon things couldn't be worse for me. And them who killed you is a-goin' free; most likely they'll never be.caught. The law or the Circle-Z'll git me, and that'll be the end of hit."

Common sense told him he gained nothing by standing there, but the thought that there might be some way out of the net stayed him. He seemed to have lost the ability to think clearly. A dozen plans which suggested themselves were dismissed immediately. Not one of them held a possibility of success. What good would it do to hide Dorr's body? He'd be missed, and the fence would tell its own story. Buckskin would be combed as soon as the storm was over.

Gault even considered taking the body to the Circle-Z; but such a course seemed hopeless.

"That would jest save my neck for the law," he argued to himself; "an' the law's all stacked ag'in me. Ain't no jury in Paradise would believe anythin' I said."

His hand flashed to his gun as he heard a man call to another, off to his right. It was Egan calling to Tiny Mears.

"I knew they wouldn't be long a-comin'," Gault muttered. "Ain't nuthin' for me to do but go. An' I guess I'll have to keep on a-goin'. They won't take me alive!"

CHAPTER III.

FLIGHT.

GAULT was a mile away by the time Race Eagan stumbled over Kit Dorr's lifeless body. The storm showed no sign of abating. Gault mumbled his thanks for that. The storm was to his liking, now, erasing his trail almost instantly. His sheep were still ahead of him. He caught up with them in the next ten minutes. They were going along without causing the dogs any further trouble. Soon the trail began to swing around the mountain into the very teeth of the wind; for over half a mile, they were a fair target for the full force of the storm, and as they climbed higher and higher, it seemed that the gale must sweep them off their feet.

To the right of the trail the mountain fell sheer to the floor of the valley. The sheep began to string out and hug the inside curve of the trail. Once or twice the dogs barked to hurry them on. Gault gave Pepper his head, but the horse could not keep up with the flock. In fact, he braced his body for every step he took and, although Gault had urgent need of haste, the horse was not to be pressed.

The snail's pace at which he rode fretted the man sorely, and it was with a keen sense of relief that he felt the horse veer off to the left some thirty minutes later. The trail widened here, and Pepper loped along. Gradually, he quartered on the wind. In a short while Gault realized that the violence of the storm had lessened. By this token, he knew they were descending the wide draw which led to the coulee. Before they reached it, Pepper caught up with the flock.

Without conscious effort, a plan of what he must do had formulated in Gault's mind. He intended to be far away by daylight; but when the sheep had been rounded up, so strong was habit in him, he stopped to help the dogs bunch the flock for the night. From his patience and the even tenor of his droning song, one would have little suspected that he had aught to hurry him.

Half an hour must have passed as he continued to circle around the flock. The old ewes were the first to heed his song. Their example had a salutary effect upon the rest of the flock, and after the rams had impressed their households with their watchfulness and superior intelligence, they, too, bedded down. The tired dogs sat about, their eyes half closed. It was sign enough that the flock was safe.

Gault did not attempt to find the trail of the man, or men, who had stampeded the sheep. The storm would have long since destroyed any sign. He knew the guilty ones were far away by now, for they would not have lingered after seeing the flock rushing down the mountain.

Pepper had not eaten since noon, and so, when Gault left the coulee, he went directly to the barn and fed the horse. Much was to depend on Pepper in the next twelve hours. He loosened the cinches of his saddle as the animal ate and, before leaving the barn, he filled a small bag with oats and fastened it to a ring in the saddlebow. If he moved slowly it was because he dreaded to face Margarida.

He had brought to her already such grief and misery as comes to few women, but the blow he was to deal her now made what had gone before seem as nothing. He knew she would meet it bravely. She ever had been the braver of the two. But why had God always demanded braveness of her? What had she done to deserve the load she had been made to carry?

And this thing to-night! Gault knew she would have to bear the brunt of it. If he got away, he would come back some day to prove himself innocent. Failing that, he had only to die, but she would have to stay here, poor, shamed—raising her son in a country where every man's hand would be raised against him. God! Was there aught of justice in this?

Gault raised his clenched fists to heaven, and a terrible oath escaped his lips. His honest, God-fearing nature had rebelled at last.

"God—if there is a God—why You a-doin' this to her?" he demanded in awful tones. "Why do You want to break her heart?—and that's what hit's a-goin' to mean! I ain't never asked nuthin' for myself; You ain't had much to do for either of us; but I'm a-askin' You now—how You a-goin' to take care of her? What You a-goin' to do for her and Joseph when I ain't here no more?—You got to look out for 'em, God! You got to take moughty good care of 'em; 'cause if Ye don't—I ain't a-goin' to believe there's any God! Don't let no man's hand touch my boy. He's clean, and You got to keep him clean! Do all You can for him and his mammy, and if You can't do nuthin' for me—I won't mind."

Margarida, worn out with anxiety, had dozed off in her chair beside the table. She sprang to her feet as her husband opened the door. "Joseph!" she cried as she ran toward him, her voice singing her relief at seeing him safely home.

Gault appeared unusually tall in the flickering rays of the lamp, his face gaunt and drawn, his eyes bloodshot from the storm. Margarida caught the grim set of his mouth and the ghostly pallor of his face. She stopped short.

"Joseph!" she exclaimed. "What has happened? What is it?"

Gault pointed to the lamp. "Put it out!" he said sharply, and as Margarida blew out the flame, he locked the door.

The ashes in the hearth were still aglow. Gault stirred them with his boot until they dimly illumined the room. The supplies for which he had gone to town were in a gunny sack thrown over his shoulder. He took the sack, and put it in the kitchen as he had always done, and coming back to the fireplace, he took several newspapers and a catalogue from his pocket and tossed them on the table.

Margarida's eyes followed him. His every move said to her that something serious had happened; but Gault, not seeing that she read him so well, tried to be casual as he spoke.

"Had trouble with the sheep," he began.

Margarida stopped him. "They were all right just before the storm, but that's not why you asked me to put out the lamp, Joseph." Her tone was accusing. Gault stared at the glowing coals.

"Yes—and—no, Rita," he muttered. "Somebody stampeded the flock. I jest managed to turn 'em this side of the fence. The fence is down—cut!"

Margarida Gault's face blanched. She grabbed her husband's arms as if she would shake from him the mystery this night held.

"You mean *our* sheep?" she demanded incredulously. "Some one stampeded our sheep and cut the Circle-Z wire so they would go through?—— Joseph!" It was a groan. Gault turned his head away.

"Don't keep me waiting," Margarida exclaimed when she could speak. "Tell me what happened! Everything!"

But she had to drag the story from him, for he was still trying to hold back word of Dorr.

"How could this have happened?" she demanded, when he had finished. "Who could have done this thing?"

"Reckon the less we say about that the better hit'll be. You and me know who done hit, but hit can't be helped."

She caught her breath as understanding flashed in her brain. Trembling, she turned to the fire. "I — I — understand, Joseph," she murmured brokenly, her voice tired, impotent. "I didn't think they would stoop to this."

Gault winced. How could he tell her what must be told? He couldn't just go. So it was with a decision born of desperation that he said tersely:

"Guess you remember Kit Dorr, Rita."

His wife nodded, surprised at the mention of Dorr's name at this time.

"Of course. But why? Had he anything to do with this?"

Gault cleared his throat nervously.

"Kit's dead—killed!"

"Ah-h-h!" There was surprise and horror in her eyes. It seemed as if by some psychic force she foresaw the dénouement of the tragedy. Her mouth hung open. It seemed to ask a question.

"I left him half buried in the sand beside the fence," Gault went on, watching her mouth.

"The fence?" Margarida's hand flew to her mouth as she backed away, her eyes bulging. "Joseph—*Joseph!*" And when Gault's eyes met hers, she stared at him madly; but he was mute. Slowly, then, a word formed on her lips:

"You—"

Gault could not answer at once. He shook his head slowly when he did speak, and his voice was hoarse:

"No-o, Rita, hit wa'n't me! I didn't kill Kit Dorr. Folks is a-goin' to say I did, though; an' there ain't no one a-goin' to believe I didn't."

"Oh, Joseph!" Margarida implored as she rushed to him and threw her arms about his neck. "Don't say that! I have never known you to lie. If you say you did not kill him, *I* believe you. Look at me, Joseph. I have faith in you!"

Gault trembled as he swept her up into his arms and kissed her.

"I haven't done much, have I, to pay you back for all the faith you've had in me?" he said brokenly.

"Joseph, my man!" Margarida repeated again and again as she clung to him.

Not until she asked to be put down did he release her.

"Joseph—do you know who shot Dorr?" she questioned.

Gault nodded: "The same folks who stampeded the sheep. Ain't no doubt of hit. Kit must a-happened along as they was cuttin' the wire."

"You—you don't think my father did this?" Margarida demanded. "He had nothing against Dorr."

"No! No, he didn't have a hand in this, but the hatred of me that he's preached all these years is to blame for hit. The Basque boys have been a-listenin' to him so long they would do anythin' to git rid of me. Dorr got hit 'cause he was in the way. The Circle-Z men must 've found Kit's body some time ago. Like as not, they'll be here, lookin' for me, 'fore mornin'. Mornin'll bring 'em, sure pop! I got to be a long ways away by then."

Margarida just nodded. She knew as well as he that his life would be snuffed out if he were caught before the excitement subsided. Yes, he had to go. And these minutes—they were too precious to be wasted. Even while they had talked, a posse might have started for the cabin. The future was black for her, but the present was beset with such danger for her husband that she dared not think of what was to become of little Joseph and herself.

"Is your horse ready?" she asked anxiously. "I'll have a snack ready for you by the time you get him. We've been foolish to stand here idle."

Gault was back with Pepper by the time she had the lunch wrapped. The storm was abating. If it held on as it was now, he would be over the mountain and well into the Owyhee country by daylight. It was his intention to go down the Little Owyhee and cross into Idaho. Beyond that, he had no definite plan.

"I ain't a-goin' to tell you where I'm headin'

for," he said huskily. "You won't have to lie to folks, then, when they try to dig hit out of you. If anybody comes to-night, say I ain't home. An' don't worry no more'n you have to, Rita. Ain't no way of sayin' how long I'll be gone. I'm a-goin' to square this, some day. The wool's contracted for; hit'll give you money enough. You'll have to git a boy for the sheep. Git word to Kincaid; he'll find a herder for you. An' if you need anythin', ask Kin; he's the only friend I got in the valley."

"Yes, yes—! Joseph," Margarida answered, "but hurry, *hurry!* What if they came now?"

"I got to kiss the baby 'fore I go," Gault mumbled, and with his wife at his heels, he tiptoed into the kitchen and opened the door of the little cubby-hole in which the child slept. The boy did not stir as his father dropped to his knees and brushed his cheek with quivering lips. Icy despair tore at Gault's heart as he gazed on his son and realized that this might be his last look at him. A mad impulse to awaken the child and hear his voice once more almost overcame the kneeling man.

Gault felt his wife's hand upon his shoulder, entreating him to delay no longer, but for a while he could not take his eyes away from the boy's face; pride and love held him chained.

Tears were denied Gault. Dry-eyed, he had to face the mother, or else even her fine courage must fail at his going. That he masked his misery was no small accomplishment.

"Don't tell him nuthin'," Gault whispered when the door had been closed, "hit'd only poison his mind. When he asks about me, tell him I had to go away for a spell. Keep this night from him as long as you can, Rita, 'cause he's gittin' so he thinks like a man; he'd want to do somethin'. And that mustn't be. I don't want him to grow up with his heart full of hate and meanness. As long as I'm alive, this is my fight; I got to settle hit myself. If anythin' happens, so I don't get back, I know you'll raise him to be a man. Teach him to—*what?*"

The sudden fear which had flashed in Margarida's eyes had forced the question from him.

"Isn't that our dogs?" she insisted.

Gault listened.

"Reckon hit is," he muttered. "Some one's a-comin'!"

"Kiss me then—quick! Put your arms about me for a second, my man. Come back to me, Joseph! I couldn't live without you. No matter when you come, I'll be here! And now, go! *Go!* They'll be here any minute!"

Gault did not mount his horse until Margarida

bolted the door. He heard something thud against it, and he wondered if she had fainted. He even ventured to call to her. When he heard her answer, he swung himself into his saddle and struck off across the mountain to the north of the coulee. The tears which had been denied him, blurred his eyes now. It did not matter; there was no one to see.

Margarida had half fallen against the cabin door as she bolted it. Valiantly, she endeavored to arrange her disordered thoughts. What was she to do when these men came? Had she been asleep?—or would it not be better to pretend that she was anxiously waiting for her husband to return from town?

As she pondered the matter, she heard horses outside the cabin. The next moment, the butt of a gun beat an angry tattoo on the door.

"Hello-o-o!" a voice cried.

"I hear you!" Margarida answered. "What is it? What do you want?"

"Open the door!"

"I'll not open the door until I know who you are!" she called back.

"I'm Eagan—Race Eagan, of the Circle-Z—I want to talk to your husband."

"My husband is not here!" she replied stoutly.

"He went to town to-day. I've been expecting him home for hours."

Eagan conferred with the other men. Then:

"Guess he'll be along directly. We got to see him. You open up and let us in. Kit Dorr's been killed. We're here to get the man that got him. What you goin' to do?"

"Wait until I light a lamp," Margarida exclaimed. "I'll let you in. There isn't anybody here who had anything to do with killing Kit Dorr."

Two other Circle-Z men were with Eagan. The three of them searched the cabin hurriedly.

"He ain't here," Race grumbled. "He's been here and gone, or he'll come soon. We'll wait a spell!"

"You think my husband killed Dorr, eh?" Margarida asked, her eyes snapping.

"What we think don't matter! We want Gault! You said he hadn't been here, didn't yuh?"

Margarida nodded: "You understood me correctly."

Eagan pulled a chair up to the table and sat down.

"Might as well sit down, boys," he said brusquely, his eyes following Margarida as she walked back and forth. He found her singularly bea:;tiful. He began to wonder about her and what was to become of her. Margarida caught his eyes and seemed to guess his thought. Eagan picked up a newspaper and read it aimlessly, still wondering about her. He stiffened suddenly.

"*Say!* I thought you was mistaken, ma'am," he exclaimed insolently. Turning to the others, he said:

"Gault was here! She's just been playin' for time."

"What do you mean?" Margarida demanded.

Eagan's lip curled as he tossed the newspaper on the table:

"I mean that there's to-day's *Silver State*. It couldn't have got to Paradise before four o'clock. How did it get here if he didn't fetch it? Ain't no airships bringin' mail up here, is there? And don't you forget that foolin' us won't help him any. Where's he headin' for?"

Eagan almost roared his question. Great was his surprise, then, to find little Joseph facing him from the kitchen door, his sleepy eyes squinting along the sights of his father's old deer-gun.

"Don't you move!" the child warned. "You wouldn't talk like that to my mammy if my daddy was here; and I reckon I ain't going to let you do it, either!"

"I'm damned!" Race drawled as he surveyed

the boy. "I *do* be damned! I guess you mean it!" He grunted as he turned to his companions:

"Come on, let's ride! And say, kid," he added as he looked at Joseph, "for your sake, I hope your paw is travelin' *fast!*"

CHAPTER IV.

ON BUCKSKIN.

WINTER, long and lonely, came to the cabin on Buckskin Mountain, but it brought no word of the husband and father who had fled in the middle of the night. In the valley, men still talked about Joseph Gault and wondered where he had gone.

That he had killed Dorr, no one doubted—save Tabor Kincaid—and his guilt was best proved by the fact that he had not waited to be hanged. In the beginning one or two dissented from this popular opinion, but as the story of Eagan's encounter with Margarida spread, they were forced to admit themselves wrong.

The killing itself was never investigated. What need for investigation, with the motive so evident and the guilty man almost self-confessed? And, so, although Dorr was soon forgotten, the hunt for Gault went on; but as time passed, and no word of him was had, the law turned to more urgent matters. And those good men and true, who had without trial judged Joseph Gault, contented themselves, with the inhumanity of man for the helpless, by openly scorning the woman and child who had been left to face them.

But Margarida's great task was not to win their approval. The wondering look which that mad, storm-filled night had put in little Joseph's eyes had never quite left them, and although she had succeeded in clouding to him the reason for his father's going, she was less successful in explaining why he remained away so long. And an uneasy feeling possessed her that he knew what had happened.

In various ways she tried to keep his mind occupied, and she spent many long hours in teaching him how to read and write. Joseph rewarded her by making astounding progress. He was going on nine, now, and actually growing out of his clothes.

Kincaid had sent them a Mexican boy to herd their sheep. He proved reliable and made himself handy about the place, but Joseph resented his being there, insisting that they could do without him.

Margarida had to smile, but it proved to her how mature his mind was. Surely a grandfather could have been proud of him. She often looked for her father to come, now that her husband was gone, but that stern man took no step in her direction. Grief had come to his home, too, but of this Margarida knew nothing. She could only wonder how he steeled his heart.

If David Gault, her husband's father, had lived, would he have been as unrelenting? The Basques had always found him an implacable foe, but she could not believe that he would have denied his own flesh at such a time as this.

Twice, during the winter, Kincaid, came. He was the only visitor. His optimism and confidence in Gault became the thread by which she clung to hope.

One morning she awakened to find the melting snow dripping from the roof of the cabin. Two weeks later, the snow had disappeared from the lower mountain. Above her, the laurel and greasewood were a blackish green against the snowy patches. Tiny rivulets raced down the mountain-side. The pungent aroma of sage-brush filled the air.

Wherever she looked life was beginning to stir. Margarida would have been less than human not to have answered in lifted spirit to the miracle being performed about her. And then, lambing-time was upon them, bringing work for all.

Joseph could not have been busier, for, in addition to the lambs, a litter of puppies had been presented to him by the coyote which Enriquez, the herder, had trapped the last winter. Margarida and the Mexican had been for dispatching the wild animal at once, but Joseph had begged to be allowed to keep it.

In a remarkably short time the dogs had ceased to take exception to the coyote. One of them was, undeniably, the father of the six brown puppies which Joseph exhibited so proudly. The elder Joseph had taken pride in his dogs, and the boy had often heard him say that they were "wolf-crossed"; in fact, he believed it was because of the wolf strain in them that they were so capable.

Little Joseph had no definite idea of what the offspring of this present *mésalliance* might develop into; but certainly his father's words inspired his hopes. Long before the puppies would drink milk from a pan, he was forcing it on them, anxious to see whether they would lap or suck it. If they lapped the milk, they were dogs; if they sucked it, the wild in them predominated, and they would most surely be sheep-killers.

Later, when they did take the milk, Joseph was unable to understand why four of them lapped it, while the other two sucked it as though they were wolf cubs. Men who have spent their lives crossing dogs with the wolf or coyote have not been able to understand it either. So, it was with a heavy heart that the two outlaws were surrendered to Enriquez.

Keeping any of the litter was a great mistake in the peon's eyes. For generations, the wolf and the coyote had been his traditional enemies. He knew that nothing good would come of keeping them, and it was madness to allow their mother to go about unchained.

Joseph's lips curled at this. What did Enriquez know about animals? He reckoned that Mexicans didn't know much about anything!

"Bet he'd laugh if I told him I'd been lugging salt all winter long to a deer up there in the rim-rocks," the lad told himself.

The herder did laugh when Joseph, getting the worst of an argument, told the story of the deer, hoping thereby to confound Enriquez.

"You wait till those coyotes wean those pup!" the Mexican scoffed. "Pretty queeck she's *go!*"

Joseph looked at him pityingly:

"Enriquez, you know nothing. I love that coyote; she loves me. She won't run away. Pretty soon I'm going to send her away, though."

The herder was not convinced. "I suppose she never eat sheep again, *qué?*"

Joseph shook his head at such stupidity:

"Sure she'll kill sheep! She's coyote, ain't she? That's why I'm going to send her away. By the time you put the sheep on the clover, the pups will be old enough to get along by themselves. Come then, I'll take old Slippy-foot over the pass, and toss a rock or two at her. Reckon she'll figure she made a mistake in picking me for a friend, but that'll be better than keeping her here until we'd have to kill her."

Time proved Joseph right, for when the pups were weaned the mother coyote followed him about like a dog. By late April, the clover was up and Enriquez was ready to move the flock. So, true to his promise, Joseph led Slippy-foot over the mountain. He came back alone; for the first time in his life he had rewarded trust and affection with a blow.

The significance of what he had done loomed larger in his mind than the deed itself. It had been necessary; but *why* had it been necessary? Even his mother's explanation failed to satisfy him. The survival of the fittest held no promise of the God he visioned.

May brought the birds to Buckskin—thrashers, woodpeckers, doves, quail, sagehen. Once more nighthawks and the whippoorwills sailed over the sage at twilight. Great flocks of crows and magpies cawed and chattered all day long. Phlox and lupine blossomed about the cabin. Where a spring dripped above the coulee, fire-red Indian-lilies nodded their heads.

Nowhere else in the world could the sky have been so blue. Rarely ever did a cloud appear. Those that came were great white clouds which floated lazily by, unhurried and bound for the far-distant Sierra. The days were long; twilight held until almost nine o'clock; then came the greatest wonder of all—the warm, yellow desert moon, turning mesa and rim-rocks into castles of silver with towers and battlements! What boy of nine could have been long unhappy there?

Joseph thrilled to it. Life was forever calling to him; not from far horizons, but right here on Buckskin. Margarida saw less and less of him as he roamed about the mountain. He brought home strange tales of his experiences with birds and animals. His mother found them hard to believe. Enriquez was even more skeptical. A few days later, however, the herder had good reason to change his mind.

It was Sunday, and even on the mountain a religious stillness seemed to mark the day. The flock was above the coulee, and Enriquez, stretched out upon the ground was watching a mob of crows circling above the draw which led toward the cabin.

Less than two hours previously he had driven

the sheep through the draw, so he knew there was nothing there for them to be feeding on; and yet, as he continued to watch them, they kept up an endless cawing. Gradually, they circled lower and lower, until Enriquez knew they had alighted. Soon the cawing stopped.

The herder's curiosity was aroused, for he fancied he knew something of the habits of crows, and experience told him this flock had descended to eat, but he knew equally well that there was no food there for them. Getting to his feet he climbed until he was high enough to see into the draw. His surprise at what he beheld rendered him speechless for a moment.

"Madre de Dios!" he exclaimed when he could use his tongue. "Joseph!—those crow ees eating out of hees han'!"

Enriquez could appreciate what he saw. He knew how next to impossible it was to get within even shooting-distance of a flock of crows. They were the wisest of all desert birds. A hundred times he had tried unsuccessfully to crawl past their sentries. But there was Joseph, standing in the center of the flock, tossing food of some kind to the hungry birds.

One crow was perched on his shoulder. Joseph would take the bird and toss it into the air, but after circling about him once or twice, it would fly back to him.

Enriquez shook his head as he watched the boy. What he beheld was almost past belief. He thought of Slippy-foot, the coyote, and of the tales of other animals which Joseph had told. He could not doubt them now. After this, he was willing to believe that the boy could do anything with wild things. But it was weird; unnatural. It savored of the devil, of black magic.

He wanted to cry out to see if the flock would rise, but a certain fear of Joseph had been born in his heart and so, although he watched until the boy went toward the cabin, he made no sound. He expected that Joseph would mention the incident that evening, but the boy said nothing.

Slippy-foot's puppies had grown into a playful, barking pack, and it became Joseph's pleasure to begin training them in the ways of sheep dogs. He found that he had set himself a task well-calculated to try the patience of youth. Summer had, passed before the older dogs would work with them.

It was necessary to move the flock daily now, and the pups had a chance to show what they had learned. Joseph was amply repaid for his faith in them, for even though they were not as patient as the old dogs they appeared able to anticipate the flock's movements more quickly. And that is the supreme test of a good sheep dog. The boy watched to see if they ever put teeth to the sheep, and when he found that they did not his last fear of the wild strain was removed.

Margarida smiled at his success, but the brightness of her eye and the roses in her cheeks were not born of health. Many times she hugged the boy to her, and Joseph did not know that the mother-spirit in her was asking him not to grow up, but to be always a boy. She knew how happy he had been this summer, and she was afraid of the future. She dreaded to think of fall and the coming winter; their gray skies and withered blossoms would be too like the bleak, hopeless misery that weighed down her heart.

But fall came on apace. The elasticity had gone from Margarida's step. Her brave mouth sagged at last. The blackness of despair had settled on her. She had been determined that, at any cost, Joseph should go to school. The wool had brought more than she had expected; it should give the boy his chance. How she was to get along without him, she did not know; but he must go.

Joseph took stoically the news of his going. Boy-like, he felt that he already had all the education he needed, that his place was here on the mountain with his mother. But when the time came, he went.

The days which followed were long ones for Margarida. It had not been her habit to tramp over the mountain, but now, in an endeavor to get away from herself, she began roaming over Buckskin. Enriquez surprised her once, standing on a ledge, her hair streaming out behind her in the wind, her eyes lighted with a strange fire. The Mexican had crossed himself as he gazed at her, silhouetted against the freshening gale. He had stolen away, wondering if she had gone mad.

He took to watching her after that day. Sub-consciously, she must have felt his eyes on her, for she no longer tramped the mountain-side about the cabin, but, instead, climbed to the very top of Buckskin.

Enriquez spied on her the day she first made the long climb to the crest. It was nearly evening when she returned. He had been blind had he not noticed her excitement. He saw her fingers clutch her apron and tear it as she stood at the stove puttering over his supper.

Her face, save for the poppies in her cheeks, was a sickly white. He read fear in every line of her. He wondered if she had actually gone mad; or had something happened to her to-day on the mountain?

That night one of the dogs came to the door of the cabin and bayed the death howl. Enriquez shivered in his blanket. He understood the dog, and knew that death was not far away. He hoped it would come before the winter snows caught him a prisoner on the mountain.

Early the next morning Margarida set out for the summit. Enriquez shook his head after she had passed. He had seen the shovel which she had tried to conceal beneath her coat. He knew, now, that she *was* insane, and as he moved about with the flock he chanted the old spirit song of the Moqui, for, in the dim past, he had sprung from Indian stock.

Margarida read the herder's thought. Had she, indeed, gone mad? She wondered. But surely, madness would have lifted the weight which bore so heavily on her. And yet, she knew that her tortured brain could stand but little more. Daily for a week, she went to the mountain-top. What the end of this would have been had not the following Saturday brought Joseph home, clothes and books, it is not hard to guess.

"Don't you be so surprised, mother," he declared. "Ain't nothing happened to me; I'm just done with school."

"But something *has* happened, Joseph," his mother exclaimed. "How did you get here?"

"I walked."

Margarida caught her breath. Whatever it was that had impelled him to do this had been no trivial thing.

"Left last night," Joseph went on. "Been coming ever since. The dogs knew me right off, didn't they?"

"No, no, Joseph!" Margarida entreated. "Don't put me off! Why did you leave? You know I want you to stay in school."

"Not in that school, mother!" the boy declared earnestly. "Folks are always talking about me in Paradise; sorta making fun of me, I reckon, 'cause I ain't got clothes like they've got. A boy commenced it yesterday, and I sassed him back. He said my daddy was a bad man. I called him a liar. Then he said his grandpa said you and my daddy wasn't married right; that you didn't have a priest. He wouldn't take it back, so I hit him. The teacher came running. But I hit him again, —'cause you did have a priest, didn't you, mother?"

Margarida was on her knees before him, her arms outstretched to enfold him.

"Come to me, my little man!" she cried. "Come to me! Let me kiss you! Of course we had a priest; but he was not the kind of priest they know in Paradise. He had no robes, but he preached the word of God, and your father and I believed in him. It didn't matter, did it, dear?"

Joseph shook his head as his mother's tears wet his face.

"And that boy, Joseph?" Margarida questioned, "you hit him hard?"

"I 'most killed him, mother!"

"Oh, I'm glad! I'm glad! And his name?"

"Juan Irosabal!" said Joseph.

Margarida winced.

"An Irosabal, eh?" In a wild fury she swept her son from his feet. *"I'm glad!"* she cried; "I'm glad you 'most killed him, Joseph!"

CHAPTER V.

TABOR KINCAID paid a visit to Buckskin shortly
after Joseph's return. His broad, usually smiling
face wore a frown, for he was the bearer of bad
news, and bad news was the last thing in the
world that he wished to carry to Margarida
Gault. His courage almost failed him as he stood
before her, her thin white hand in his.

She smiled bravely at him, but his keen eyes
were not deceived, and he prayed that she might
not see the surprise her appearance caused him.
It was hard for him to believe that she was the
Margarida Gault, who as a bride, had come to
Buckskin such a few years ago.

Kincaid kept back the news which had brought
him up the mountain, and it was not until he was
ready to leave that he broached it. Then with
that indirection which appears to belong only to
desert men, he spoke.

"Did Joe ever try to buy this land?" he asked.

"He often spoke of it," Margarida answered.
"But that was before it was put in the Forest

Reserve. For the last three years we have been paying a grazing fee; ten cents a head this year, not counting the lambs."

"Forest Reserve!" Kincaid exclaimed with biting sarcasm. "Did it ever strike you as strange that Buckskin should have been included in a reserve? They ain't enough timber on this mountain to build a man a house—stunted cedar and mountain mahogany, and maybe a piñon pine or two, don't sound to me like much of a beginning for a forest reserve. No sir-ree!

"The way public lands have been juggled around in this state is something scandalous. The State Land Office has been swapping good for bad so long that they've pretty near run out of good things. Somebody has been casting eyes at Buckskin. The Surveyor-General restored it to the public domain last week."

"You mean the mountain is no longer a part of the Forest Reserve?" Margarida asked anxiously.

"It was thrown open to entry last week. It was filed on immediately—almost, I might say, before the dear general public knew about it. It went for a dollar and a quarter an acre. I could have used it."

Margarida began to understand what Kincaid was telling her. At first, his matter-of-fact tone had not aroused any sense of suspicion in her, and she had not been prepared for what he had just told her.

"Do I understand that Buckskin has been sold?" she demanded, her voice strange to her ears.

Kincaid nodded.

"Your father bought it in."

The big man was watching her covertly, and he reached out his hand to catch her as he saw her lean against the cabin door for support.

A startled, "Oh!" was Margarida's only answer, her weary brain refusing to grasp the full significance of what she had heard.

"He won't be able to take possession until the first of the year," Kincaid went on. "But the snow will be here then. I suppose he won't ask you to go before spring. Even so, you and the boy had better come down to my place for the winter. I had this in mind when I spoke a while back about your coming."

Margarida shook her head determinedly:

"You are very kind. Please do not think we fail to appreciate what you have done. But my place is here. I promised my husband that he would find me waiting for him. Why, I can not say, but he has seemed near me these last days. When he comes, he will find me. My father has

left nothing undone to break my heart; let it remain for him to drive me away."

And although Kincaid was persistent, urging
her health as a reason for accompanying him, he
went back to the valley alone. Somehow her saying her husband seemed near lingered in his mind
even after he had reached his ranch. He did not
doubt that her spirit was wandering already into
the limitless void, straightening its wings for the
great flight to those sublime heights from which
it could commune with the missing loved one.

Joseph found his mother in tears on the evening of Kincaid's visit. She told him what had
occurred. The effort exhausted her. Enriquez
and he carried her to her bed.

Margarida's magnificent will had always sustained her; that it had failed her at last, filled
her with fear. Her body had long been weary,
but she had willed it on; and now her will was
weary. With the knowledge came hopelessness,
for the props on which she had leaned had been
built on her will; over night they came tumbling
down like a house of cards.

The following day she had her bed moved so
that she could look across the mountain. She
knew that the end was near. Out there, somewhere, was the man she loved. She wondered if
he was waiting for her, or had her spirit called to

him in the flesh and turned his feet in her direction?

Sometime, somewhere, they must meet again! It could not be otherwise. With the thought, a great peace came to her. Resignation robbed her eyes of their wistfulness, painting in them a light of happiness, of coming glory.

For hours at a time Joseph sat beside her, his eyes ever on her face. He knew nothing of death, save as he had seen it in the wild; but he knew something tremendous was about to happen, something bigger than anything he had known. It kept his throat tight and stabbed at his heart.

"Daddy ought to be here, mother," he said to her. "He'd know what to do. I'm only a boy, and I don't know how to get you well. You're always smiling when you look at me, but I know there's something inside of you that hurts. Maybe I'd better make Enriquez go for Tabor Kincaid. If anybody could get a doctor, he could."

"Mother doesn't need a doctor, dear," Margarida whispered to him.

"Enriquez says we ought to get a priest," Joseph went on. His mother drew his face close to hers:

"No—no, Joseph! Enriquez is mistaken. But maybe you'd better send for Mr. Kincaid. Tell Enriquez to take the horse and go."

Margarida seldom closed her eyes. Whenever she did, Joseph pulled off his boots and crept about the cabin in his stocking feet. Sometimes, through half closed eyelids, his mother watched him as he moved about doing what he could for her. Once, when he thought her asleep, she heard him "talking to God," as he called it.

After that, she often "talked to God;" but it was of Joseph, and not of herself, that she spoke. What was to become of him? Dared she hope that her father would care for him? Reason said no; but if she sent Joseph to him now, could he refuse to come to her?

What message could she send that would bring him?—and a voice whispered; "The secret on the mountain-top!"

Yes, she told herself, that was it! Angel Irosabal could not deny that summons. She had kept the secret well, but as she called Joseph to her side when Enriquez had gone, and gave him the message for her father, she promised herself that if he failed to come to her, Joseph should have the secret of Buckskin.

Her own life had been laid waste by hatred, but she had tried to hide it from her son. Even so, had she kept from him the story of the injustice done his father. Her husband had asked that. A legacy of hate was a poor heritage, but she could not ask her son to always turn the other cheek.

Never before had she asked her father's mercy. She was on her knees to him now. If he failed her, it must be for Joseph to right the wrong which had been done his father and her.

Since babyhood, in Joseph's eyes, Angel Irosabal's *caserio* had been an ogre's castle. The bad man of his dreams lived there, but it was with a brave smile to his mother that he set forth. He knew he must go swiftly. The trail which Enriquez had taken to the valley was not to be thought of, for Joseph had no horse. An old deer run led down the side of the mountain, and that was the course he took.

Margarida knew it would be morning before he could return with her father. At dawn her eyes were open, searching the mountain-side for them. She knew they must come soon, or else be too late. Her spirit waited only for them.

It must have been eight o'clock when she thought she saw a speck moving up the mountain. Weak as she was, she pulled herself into a sitting position and watched the running, jumping object that was surely hurrying hurrying toward the cabin. It was Joseph! And he was alone! Angel Irosabal had turned him from his door!

Margarida wished that she might call out to

Joseph and bid him not to hurry, for, no matter how fast he ran, he would be too late. Never again would their mortal eyes behold each other.

An hour later, tired and hollow-eyed, the boy reached the cabin. Twice he raised his hand to open the door before he found courage to do it. He called to Margarida, but there was no response. Rushing to her side, he clutched her hands; they were still warm. For an instant he took hope, and shook her faintly. And then he knew!—his mother was dead!

He had left the door open and Brindle, his favorite of Slippy-foot's pups, had followed him into the cabin. The dog put his paws upon the bed and nuzzled Margarida's hand. Joseph hugged the dog, and as Brindle threw back his head and voiced the misery that was in him, the boy sobbed out his grief.

Time passed unnoticed. Here was the end of all things. What good to go to the door and see if Enriquez was returning with Tabor Kincaid? The dogs were barking; perhaps the sheep were in trouble—Joseph shook his head. The sheep mattered not.

How long he knelt beside his dead mother before he became aware of his slate, propped against the wall, he did not know. Only yesterday he had used it. He saw the pencil lying upon the coverlet, where it had evidently fallen from his mother's fingers. And then, before he fully realized that the slate held a message for him, he was reading it:

My Joseph:
I can see you, my son. You are running, but your little legs will not bring you to me in time. Leave Buckskin. Go where you can grow into the man I know you can be. Some day, when you are grown, you must come back here. You have got to right a great wrong. On the very top of the mountain you will find your answer. Let this be your secret, my Joseph. Your fa——

The last two lines were so faint the boy read them with difficulty. Brindle stared at him quizzically. Word by word, he committed the message to memory. The dog stiffened at the sound of Enriquez's voice. Joseph heard Kincaid, too. They must have hurried to have come so soon.

He put the slate upon his knees, and with the sleeve of his coat rubbed out his mother's words. He wished they had not come just yet, for he wanted to be alone. He grabbed his hat and walked to the door as Kincaid knocked.

Joseph's eyes told their own story.

"I'm mighty sorry, Joseph," Kincaid muttered. "The Doc was off to Quinn River, but I guess he couldn't have done nothing."

Joseph nodded dumbly.

"You go off up the mountain for a spell," Kincaid went on. "I'll do what I can here."

Later, in a crude coffin of his own making, he and Joseph buried Margarida. Enriquez looked from one to the other—the burial left nothing undone. What was to become of him? Kincaid caught the herder's questioning look; he wondered, too. It was necessary that he go back to his own ranch. Something definite must be done about Joseph. That night he spoke to him about the future.

"You can't stay here, my boy," Kincaid said.

"I'm not aiming to stay here," Joseph answered. "My grandpa can have the place. Guess the best thing for me to do is to roll up a few things and go."

"The sheep are yours, Joseph. Irosabal didn't get them thrown in when he bought the mountain. How many head do you reckon on?"

"Nigh four hundred," the boy replied without any show of interest. He couldn't take the sheep along with him to the vague and distant land to which he was going.

"The market's about six dollars a head now," Kincaid muttered, busy with his pencil. "That won't be so bad. If you say so, I'll sell the sheep for you. It'll give you enough to get a decent education, Joseph."

Joseph shook his head at the word education. Kincaid shook his head, too:

"I don't mean *Paradise*. When I say education, I mean back East—Chicago, or some place like that. You know, Joseph, your daddy just about saved my life once. He'd never let me do anything to pay him back. I swear he must have been waiting to have me do it for *you* instead of *him*. Ain't no one been near you but me. Don't seem as if any one cared what happened to you, but old Tabor Kincaid.

"I'd adopt you, Joseph, sure as shooting, if I thought your grandpap would let me. The law don't give me any right to sell your sheep—you being a minor, and me no legal guardian of you, but I'm going to do it. I won't see old Angel grab them, and have you bound out to boot!

"Maybe he'll make me some trouble, but he'll find he ain't fighting a ten year old boy and his mammy. But we ain't got no time to waste, Joseph. What do you say?"

"You been most like a daddy to me, since mine went away," the little fellow replied cautiously. "I reckon I'd be pretty mean not to do as you say. But I've got to come back here some day. I've got something to do here that I mustn't never forget."

"I guess I know what you mean," Kincaid murmured. "And I'm not saying you shouldn't come back. But I want you to come back a man, Joseph."

"That's what my mother said," Joseph agreed. "And I reckon that's the way I'm coming back."

CHAPTER VI.

THE UNKNOWN PRESENCE.

THERE are two roads by which one may enter Paradise Valley from the north. The more traveled one cuts through the Santa Rosa Forest Reserve and, after swinging around the face of Hinkey Summit, drops into the valley in a series of easy grades. The other road curves to the east, skirting Buckskin, and does not turn north until it strikes Antelope Springs.

In May, when the herds and flocks are going into the Reserve for the summer, both roads are ground to powder beneath the hoofs of countless sheep and cattle. A saddle, or low hog-back, connects Buckskin with the Santa Rosa range. A trail traverses the saddle—a short cut with a saving of many miles for one traveling north or south.

In times past, Angel Irosabal's herders—his sons and his grandsons—had made use of that short cut across the mountain, but this particular spring, as if by common consent, they avoided it. For three weeks the Basque herders had been going north, driving not less than fourteen thousand sheep.

In the late afternoon of this day—the twenty-first of May, to be exact—a slowly moving dust cloud hovered above the yellow road. It marked the progress of the last flock of the year on its way to the high hills of the Reserve. This band was not a large one, and the two herders in charge of it wallowed along in the dust unconcernedly.

One of the two was only a slip of a boy, the other a black-visaged man, heavy of jaw and narrow-eyed. When they spoke, which was seldom, they addressed each other in Basque.

"Is it far to the spring, Andres?" the boy asked. Getting no answer, he repeated his question.

The man grunted: "Thirsty?"

The boy nodded. "The dust," he said tersely.

"We will reach it by sundown," Andres said with his habitual gruffness. "Maybe it will be dry," he went on, as much to himself as to the boy.

For all that the man was the lad's uncle, the boy half feared the surly Andres. Not for some time did he venture another question.

"What will we do if it is dry?" he asked at last.

Andres grinned as he glanced at the youth.

"You are afraid, eh, Felipe?" he demanded tauntingly. The boy winced, and Andres laughed.

"If it's dry, we'll dig it out!" he exclaimed. "A little mud will not hurt you."

Felipe's throat was parched, and the prospect of having to quench his thirst with a cupful of riled water incensed him.

"Well do you say that we may find it dry," he muttered petulantly. "We are the very last. If we had taken the short cut over Buckskin we would have had plenty of water."

"You bleat now, eh?" Andres remarked hotly. "This morning you talked out of the other side of your mouth. It was to please you that we followed the road. I made no talk about ghosts."

"No, but you were glad that I did," Felipe replied with a show of truculence quite new in him. "You were none too anxious to cross Buckskin."

"Are you saying that I was afraid?" Andres demanded angrily. "This talk of ghosts is the cackling of children."

"I did not use the word," Felipe retorted. "But something is living up there. All of this talk does not spring from nothing. Lope says that he saw him; says he was within a hundred yards of him."

"I've heard his story. Why did he run away? Lope is a coward! I don't believe he saw any one.

If he did, why didn't he go up and talk to him and find out his business. The Irosabals can't use the range up there, but a stranger in rags can, eh? Lope says that the man he saw had sheep."

"Only fifteen or twenty head."

"Even so; your grandfather has heard Lope's tale. Has he done anything about it? Of course not! He is not fooled."

"No?" Felipe queried. "Perhaps grandfather sees ghosts up there that we know little about."

Andres's eyes narrowed shrewdly as he glanced at the boy.

"It would not be well for you to let him hear you say that," he warned.

Felipe shook his head slowly. "I am not afraid," he declared. "He knows what I think. One day I caught him kneeling beside that grave on Buckskin. I asked him why he knelt there, and he snarled at me, but he would not answer—as if an answer were necessary. He has admitted to himself what he will not admit to us.

"What has the mad hatred that he has always preached gained for us? What happened in the past, belongs in the past. If our people were abused when they came here, it was partly their fault. But you are like your father, Andres."

"Yes, and you would do well to think as I do. I hate these gringos, these *criollos!* Why do they give themselves the airs they do? Haven't we proved ourselves good citizens?"

"We've proved ourselves able to do everything but forgive and forget an injustice!" Felipe answered boldly. "It was well enough to remember, when we were only a few, but we are many now; and we're here for all time. There's no more talk of Spain. I'm a man—"

"A man?" Andres cried with a fine sarcasm. "You're nothing but a boy, with your face as soft as a girl's! You'll do what you are told to do. Who cares what you think? Don't let me hear any more of your foolish mouthings. Do you understand?"

Andres glared menacingly at the boy, his neck muscles bulging with anger. Felipe knew that Andres was a bully, and previous experiences had taught him the wisdom of walking wide of the man's powerful hands, so he contented himself in the present instance by turning away with a scornful grunt.

Felipe's gesture stung Andres, and he continued to watch the boy as they went along, waiting expectantly for him to voice the hot words that trembled on his tongue. Felipe, however, was not to be goaded into battle with Andres, and it was not until they reached the spring that he spoke again.

"Well, it's dry!" he exclaimed angrily.

Andres scowled as he surveyed the spring. Both of them cursed their luck in their own way.

"Don't stand there doing nothing," Andres snapped. "Unpack the burro, and get me a shovel. The ground is still wet. I'll dig a hole. We'll have water in an hour."

Felipe did as he was bidden to do and later, with the help of the dogs, he got the flock to bed down. On returning to the spring, he found Andres staring moodily at the hole which he had dug. An inch of water had seeped into it already, but it was heavy with silt and covered with an oily scum. Unpalatable as it looked, it was water, and the sight of it maddened the boy. He threw himself to the ground to drink, but Andres shouldered him away.

"You can't drink it yet," he grumbled. "It will settle in a short while."

Felipe's eyes flashed, and he longed to strike Andres, but he dropped back to wait in sullen silence for the water to clear.

Twilight fell as they waited, but neither offered to build a fire. Some minutes later the dogs barked and, on getting to his knees, Felipe made out the figure of a man approaching the spring. In his hand the man held a lead rope, and behind him shuffled a decrepit pack horse.

Andres caught the query in Felipe's eyes, and he got up and stared at the figure approaching from the north.

"Old man Organ," he muttered irritably on recognizing him. Without bothering to conceal his annoyance at being discovered camped beside the muddy spring when fresh water was only an hour's journey away, he sank back again to his former position.

Peter Organ was a very old man. He had tramped the Nevada hills years before the first Basque had set foot in the state. He was one of the few left of those who had seen the first Basques trek into the country of the Humboldt. From Angel down, they had no fault to find with old Peter.

But then, he was of the kind who find virtue in a Digger Indian with quite the same ease that most men find it in prince or bishop. Likewise, his ability at recognizing men's faults had become proverbial, and backed up with a sharp tongue it had given him a certain prominence which, otherwise, would have been denied to him.

Hair had long since ceased to adorn his bald pate, and even his stubby white beard seemed to have been nipped by the many adventurous years he had lived. His eyes, however, were keenly alive, and they twinkled mischievously as they beheld Andres and his nephew.

"Howdy-do, boys!" he exclaimed. "Had to dig her out, eh?" he inquired with provoking inflection. "I'm ashamed of you, Andres, coming here this late in the month lookin' fer water, especially since you knew all the others had gone up ahead of you." Peter snorted as he viewed the water which had seeped into the freshly-dug hole.

"You ain't a-goin' to drink that mess, be yuh?" he asked.

Andres stirred uncomfortably.

"Eet's all right, by'm-by," he argued.

"Sure!" Peter agreed. "I've drunk worse 'an that; an' sometimes I ain't drunk nuthin'; but not when there was good water three er four miles away."

"Where ees that good water, *señor?*" Felipe asked eagerly.

"That big spring above the coulee on Buckskin," Peter answered rather sharply.

Felipe's face fell, and Andres muttered something to himself.

"Buckskin?" the old man queried. "What's wrong with it?—oh—!" And he grinned impudently. "I'd clean fergot that you boys was walkin' wide of the mountain." He glanced at Andres.

"I didn't think they'd scare *you* away," he added.

Andres grumbled and got to his feet.

"I come theese way to please heem," he asserted angrily, pointing to Felipe.

"Yeh?" Peter queried as if doubting the truth of Andres's words, and he turned his shrewd old eyes on the boy for confirmation or denial of the statement. Felipe winced as he felt the old man's questioning glance.

"Eet's always my fault eef something go wrong," he muttered as he turned his face away.

"But what *is* all this talk?" Peter demanded. "What's this wild tale that young Lope's been tellin'?"

"Andres pretends to laugh at eet, *señor*," Felipe announced with evident relish. "All spring long we know something ees on the mountain. Many time we see where the grass ees eaten off. We run no sheep up there, so we look around and try find what eet ees. Not once do we see anytheeng. Then Lope ees find where some one make many fires. Andres say maybe that's you make those fire."

Peter shook his head. "I ain't crossed the mountain since the snow went off," he declared.

Felipe paused to let Andres deny this, but Andres was silent for once.

"Then one day Benito ees coming down the mountain. Eet was almost dark, and sometheeng ees chase heem. He run very fast, but he say he hear somtheeng pant right behind heem. He ees afraid to look and see what eet ees, and then he heard a laugh. Eet make heem shiver, he say.

"After that no one go up the mountain for long time, until Lope and I go. You know where that grave ees in the cedars! Well, my grandfather have that fence and monument taken down many years ago; but for some reason, Lope and I look there, and *Virgen santisima!*—that monument ees back; that fence ees there!"

Old Peter's expression had changed as the boy went on.

"What did Angel say to that?" he asked.

"He was very angry, and he told us to keep off the mountain. But my brother, Tomas, he not believe that story about the monument, and he start up Buckskin. Before he get half way, he fall seeck, and everybody say some bad spirit on the mountain make heem seeck."

"Fool talk—fool talk;" Andres growled.

"*Si! Si!*—fool talk!" Felipe retorted. "But you never try to find out what ees up there. No one ees try until Lope goes. Lope saw heem. He's a man, weeth long hair way down to hees shoulder. Lope say he look like the Christ. Hees shirt ees all open, and he ain't got no shoes. He carry beeg staff like old-time Basque shepherd. And hees eye— Lope say he tremble all over when that man look at heem."

"Umm," old Peter muttered as if weighing the boy's words. "What's he doin' up there? Did Lope find out?"

"He'es got maybe twenty head of sheep."

Twenty head, in a land where sheep are counted by the thousand, gave no inkling of the man's real business.

"That don't explain nuthin'," Peter declared.

"Maybe eet explain somtheeng when I tell you he'es got a coyote to herd those sheep!" Felipe exclaimed this with the air of one who drops a verbal bombshell.

"Naw!— I ain't never heard tell of such a thing." Peter was openly skeptical.

"Ain't no man ever trained a coyote so he wouldn't tech sheep."

Andres added his doubting grunt to the old man's frank disbelief in the possibility of training a coyote.

"Well, he'es done eet," Felipe answered. "I'm telling the truth."

"*Oh, callate!*" Andres exclaimed wearily. "The truth?—humph! You say only what that fool Lope says, fit cackle for old women and children. For me, I think eet's all damn foolishness."

"*So?*" Felipe queried mockingly. "What you make of that, then?" And he pointed to a flickering fire far up the side of Buckskin.

All three squinted their eyes as they focused them on the distant camp-fire. Peter saw Andres's face pale. Felipe's pointing hand trembled. The old man glanced at them and then back at the tiny point of fire.

"It's jest about at the spring," he muttered. Out of the tail of his eye he saw Felipe cross himself. An unintelligible oath escaped Andres. Peter rubbed his chin meditatively with the back of his hand.

"Come on, Snowball," he snapped at last, addressing his horse, "ain't no ghosts or nuthin' scarin' us. We're a-goin' up thar!"

CHAPTER VII.

THE lonely cañons and solitudes, which old Peter had plumbed, had left their mark on him, and in many ways he was more an Indian than a white man. He was not only superstitious, but he shared the red man's fear of the Unknown, and as he toiled up the hog-back which led toward the coulee his mind was busy with Felipe's tale. Just how much of it he was to believe was a question. For a month or more, at odd intervals, he had heard many strangely garbled stories about the man who lived on Buckskin.

At first he had laughed at them, but lately he had taken them seriously enough. Quite unknown to himself, a certain fixed idea regarding the identity of the mysterious stranger had crept into his mind.

"It must be him—come back after all these years," he mused aloud as he went along. "I always reckoned he would come back if they didn't catch him. I guess I'll know him if anybody would. Yes, sir. Poor old Kit Dorr. Kit wa'n't a bad boy, in his way. Ten or twelve years he's been dead now." Peter clucked his lips as he let his mind run over those lost days.

"Reckon no one but me and old Angel, and one other, really knows who got Kit," he mused on after a while. "And now *he's* come back to square things—Joe Gault! It must be him that's up thar—or shucks!—maybe it's just a ha'nt come to plague old Angel."

Peter laughed immoderately at his own thought. He stopped abruptly, however, as the raucous cawing of a crow reached his ears. That call, coming after dark, was an ominous sign. Peter waited until the echoes which it awakened had died away before he went on.

Why, he could not have told (he had climbed this hog-back a hundred different nights), but a feeling of impending evil clutched him. As he reached the divide that dropped away to the draw in which the herder's cabin had once stood, he droned a dismal chant, half savage in its wild rhythm.

Now was that peculiar moment just before moonrise when the night is darkest, and Peter and his aged horse were only a grayish blur against the swaying sage. Ten minutes sufficed to bring them to the coulee.

Suddenly the warning yip-yip of a coyote shattered the stillness of the young night. Peter's lips became mute as he listened. A wild coyote always calls more than once, but no succeeding bark came now.

Snowball, the horse, was quite used to coyotes, and he continued to shuffle along, Peter at his side. Not until they were half way across the coulee did the old man catch sight of the tiny fire beside the spring. On the grassy plain before him, and dimly outlined by the distant fire, a small band of sheep munched the grass contentedly.

Peter's eyes, however, were focused on the fire, and in another step or two he made out a man standing beside it, his head turned in the old man's direction. It was evident from the pose of his body that the coyote's bark had warned him that some one was approaching, and that he waited now for whoever was on the coulee to come up to his fire.

Peter was still some yards away, but his keen eyes saw that the man beside the fire was but a youth. He recalled Lope's description of him. Indeed, this boy might have stepped out of the Bible.

"But he's only a kid," Peter muttered to himself, taken back. "Joe Gault would be nigh on fifty by now."

As he came nearer he felt the spell of the

youth's piercing black eyes. The reddish-brown hair which fell to his shoulders seemed to accentuate the thinness of his cheeks, still covered with the silken down of adolescence. And yet, for all its thinness, the boy's face—the set of his mouth, particularly—hinted of strength,—strength with the flexibility of finely tempered steel.

His clothes were old and torn; but they were clean. His open shirt revealed a wind-tanned chest, the skin as smooth as velvet. His arms were almost bare and, man-fashion, Peter's eyes turned to them, watching the play of the rippling muscles as the boy straightened up.

"Howdy!" the old man exclaimed by way of greeting. "Seen your fire from below. Mind if I lay out here to-night?"

The other's face relaxed at old Peter's request.

"You are welcome," he said simply, "not only to the spring, but to such food as I have to offer you." His words were well turned and the tone of his voice was quite foreign to the desert-born. Peter noted the difference.

"I'm obleeged to you," he declared as he led Snowball up to the spring. The boy had turned his attention to the pot simmering upon the fire. Peter's eyes took advantage of the movement to scan the crude dug-out which the youth had contrived.

The face of the mountain rose in an overhanging ledge and, by using it for back wall and roof, it had been necessary to construct only two sides and an entrance way. This had been so well done with sod and rock that the dug-out would have offered fair shelter against even the severe storms of winter.

An unhung door—to be put in place at the owner's will—leaned against the front wall. Glancing into the interior of the dug-out, Peter saw an old table and chair, salvaged doubtlessly from the cabin which had once stood on the mountain-side. Makeshifts served in lieu of other necessities. Everything seemed to say that the place had been occupied for some time.

The boy had risen and entered the dug-out as Peter busied himself with his horse, and he came to the door now and spoke to the old man.

"We will eat, my friend," he said briefly.

Friend was a word that old Peter used very cautiously and then only after careful observation. He raised his eyebrows at hearing it on this young stranger's lips. The boy saw the question that flashed in his eyes.

"I depend on other eyes and ears than mine for the use of the word," he said frankly. "Had I not known that you came as a friend, I would have found means to prevent your coming."

The quiet confidence with which this statement was made rather upset old Peter, and it was with a feeling almost of awe that he entered the dug-out.

"Well, I'm right glad to hear you say so, any-how," he mumbled as he took the chair offered him. "It may git to that some day, between us; your voice kinda gives me hope. Folks has been a-sayin' they was a ha'nt up here. You can't git those Basque boys to come up the mountain."

For all of the apparent indirectness of his words they carried a question, and when he looked up he found the boy's eyes peering into his own. They did not waver as he waited to reply.

"It is well," he said at last, and the flat finality of his words robbed Peter of any desire to pursue the matter further. In fact, not until he had fin-ished his supper did the old man speak again.

"Ain't a bad place you've got here," he drawled. "You can see a lot of country from this coulee—old Angel Irosabal's *caserio* and all those other Basque *ranchos* down in the valley." Peter was still asking questions without appear-ing to, and he watched the boy's face as he ran on; but the young stranger gave no sign of being aware that the old man's words carried an intimation.

"You know, it kinda upset me meetin' you up

here this-a-way," Peter began again. "I'd had my mind all set on meetin' some one else."

He pushed back his chair and, tilting it upon its hind legs, he teetered to and fro, pursing his lips idly as he tamped down the tobacco in his stubby old pipe. His air of ease, however, was studied and his eyes did not lose their alertness. He wanted to draw the boy out. Naturally, he had expected him to show some curiosity about the statement which he had just made; but in this he was disappointed, for the young stranger's face remained emotionless, and there was no note of eagerness in his voice as he said:

"Yes?"

Peter could not help but feel that even such mild inquisitiveness had been prompted only by politeness. He was not offended, however. In fact, quite the reverse was true for the boy was exhibiting those very qualities which the old man prized most. Hence, it was without guile that he said:

"Yep! Reckon you wouldn't know him. Just a whim of mine. But when Angel's boys began telling me they was some one up here, I figgered if they *was* there must be some reason for it. And I ain't got along this far without sizin' up one or two things in life. No, sir! If they's anything a man remembers it's hate and revenge—

not sayin' it's right, but it just seems to eat in on some folks. I've seen a-plenty of what's gone on around here. Lord, man! I remember things—"

Peter shook his head as he gazed back at the years. "Why, I knew Angel Irosabal when he wa'nt nuthin' more than a lad like you." He paused and then, more to himself than to the boy, he murmured, "Reckon he ain't grcwn up, yet."

Peter's rambling talk caught and held the youth's attention, and with his arms resting on the table before him he waited for the old man to continue, but some minutes passed in silence before Peter went on.

"Lookin' back that-a-way," he mused aloud, "it wa'nt hard for me to recollect the name of a man who had somethin' to come back here for. He left this country in a hurry—between darkness and dawn—and he ain't never been heard of since. He used to live here on the mountain. His name was Joe Gault."

"You—knew him?" the boy questioned. Peter thought his voice sounded strained.

"Y-e-s-s-s," he drawled. "I reckon I began traipsin' over this mountain soon after it was built. Leastwise, I was here long before he came. Many's the night I stopped at his cabin. Used to stand right over thar in the draw." Peter lifted his hand and indicated the spot.

"Ain't nuthin' left of it now," he continued. "Old Angel had it torn down long ago so it wouldn't remind him of things he's been a-tryin' to fergit for nigh on twenty-five years." Peter stopped abruptly and brought his chair down upon all four legs. "Listen to me run on!" he exclaimed. "Am I a-wearyin' yuh?"

The boy shook his head solemnly.

"No, my friend," he said, "I pray you, go on."

And so, in colorful fashion, old Peter told him the story of Joseph and Margarida Gault. Before he had finished, he found the boy hanging on his words.

"But five or six months before Kit Dorr was killed, Gault and me fell out," Peter was saying, "and when I went north that spring I passed here in the night so nobody'd be embarrassed none. I'd always got along pretty well with Angel, and Gault thought I was tryin' to patch things up—which I was; meddlin' like old fools do where they ain't got no business to—and it set him dead ag'in me.

"I was rammin' around the Jacksons, way up in Idaho, all that summer. Didn't find nuthin' up thar, so I started back along in August, and it jest so happened that I camped along that hog-back the very night Dorr was killed. The storm soon drove me down below.

"Maybe you recollect seein' that pocket jest this side of that old deer run?—well, I curled up thar, and didn't move until the posse combed me out the next mornin'. Joe hadn't lit out none too soon, for they wa'nt askin' if he was guilty."

Peter's pipe had long been out, but he paused now to waste another match on the ashes it held.

"You know," he said, thoughtfully, "I couldn't go to that cabin the next day and face his wife, her knowing that Joe and me had fallen out— and her needin' some one, too. But I got a man up here in a hurry to look after 'em. He was a true friend. He couldn't do much, though.

"Margarida just faded away and died. Folks said it was consumption, but just between you and me it was a broken heart that killed her. And there was that boy of hers left all alone. My friend Tabor took him; packed him off to school, back East. God did a good job when he made Tabor Kincaid. And now, he's gone, too."

Peter glanced up to find the stranger's face hard, unlovely, his mouth cruel.

"And the boy?" he prompted huskily.

"Why, according to Tabor, the lad took sick and died years ago. The Basques were always pesterin' Kincaid about him, and I used to think

Tabor had given out that story jest to git rid of 'em. But I reckon a man can't rightly question him now; it's been too long ago."

The old man was silent for a long time after he had finished. The boy had got up, and he stood in the doorway now looking out across the coulee. After some minutes, he said, without turning to face Peter:

"And the boy's father—you have never had any word of him?"

"Nary a word. I always figgered he got down to the *Rio Colorado* some way, and followed it clear into Sonora."

"And yet," said the youth at the door, "you expected to meet him here to-night?"

"Well, if ever a man had anythin' to square, it's Joe Gault. I ain't never believed for a minute but what he'd come back. He's got that stubborn Kaintucky blood in him—it never fergits. And he knows what I know—he didn't kill Kit Dorr."

With savage swiftness the stranger whirled on Peter. The old man met his eyes squarely.

"Can you prove that statement?" the boy demanded, his voice charged with emotion.

Peter chuckled softly to himself.

"I thought that would surprise you," he replied deliberately.

"Yes?" the youth questioned, and the old man found his eyes as cold as snow-capped mountains. "You have not answered me," he insisted.

"No. But what I said is easily proved."

"And yet you refuse to speak," the stranger said bitterly. "You call yourself his friend— you have allowed these many years to pass without raising your voice to clear his name? You shame the word friend."

It was a cry of despair. The boy's voice hung on in the little room, ominous and dreadful. Peter drew back in spite of himself. As he did so he saw a tawny shape bound into the dugout.

In a daze, he saw the slavering white fangs, and felt the hot breath of the crouching, bristling thing on the floor before him. Instinctively, he reached for his gun.

"Down!" the boy commanded. "Down, Slippy-foot!"

Slowly the big coyote backed away from Peter. For the first time he recognized it for what it was. The animal had flashed at him so suddenly out of the darkness that his hands still trembled as he fingered his gun. The coyote was old; not less than fifteen years. It glared at him now with the savage ferocity of a wolf.

"So that's your *dog*, eh?" the old man muttered shakily.

"I am sorry," the boy said. "She is a faithful friend. I did not think of her when I raised my voice in anger to you. I ask your pardon."

"You was makin' pretty strong medicine for me," Peter grinned as he brushed his lips with his hand. "That animal been tendin' those sheep?"

The old man shook his head incredulously as the boy nodded.

"I never expected to live to see that," he said. "She ain't a cross, neither. What's that you call her?"

"Slippy-foot."

"Humph! Strange—mighty strange," Peter mused aloud. "I've heard tell that animals don't fergit."

The youth gazed at the old man shrewdly, and although he sensed the note of intimation in Peter's words he preferred to let it go unnoticed.

"You are a very old man," said he. "Your days may be numbered even now. Are you going to take your secret to the grave with you?"

"You ain't none too cheerful, be yuh?" Peter said with a sly grin. "I intend to go on livin' for years and years. But seriously, now, I was thinkin' about that very thing on my way up here to-night. Ain't no man ever heard what you call my secret, but Kincaid—I reckon if anybody ought to hear it, it's you."

The youth could not repress a sudden start.

"Man," he exclaimed, "you talk in riddles."

"I'm not so sure of that," Peter said, and he got to his feet. "The time's come for you and me to be frank. I've been doin' a heap of thinkin' while I been sittin' here. I knew I'd seen your eyes and mouth before. They belong to Margarida Gault. When you called that thar animal Slippy-foot, I knew I wa'n't mistaken. Boy—I reckon I know who you are. I ain't never liked no one better. Thar's my hand."

The young stranger silently stared at Peter. Seconds passed, and he did not move, but slowly his eyes softened.

"I believe you do," he whispered.

"You are Joe Gault's boy—" A mist was in old Peter's eyes. As from a distance he saw the youth nod and heard his softly uttered:

"Yes; I am Joseph."

CHAPTER·VIII.

EVEN UNTO THE LOWEST.

With that peculiar reticence of men who lead lonely lives, old Peter refrained from asking the many questions which rushed to his tongue. That the lad was Joseph, here in the flesh and not dead, surprised him less than may be imagined.

The manner of the boy's coming, his strange dress, the return of the coyote—these were matters of far greater interest at the moment. In fact, they occupied Peter's attention so fully that many minutes passed before he spoke of that storm-tossed night when Kit Dorr was killed.

"Joseph," he said solemnly, "I am afeerd that what I'm a-goin' to tell you will lead to more killin's—you bein' here this-a-way. I see it in your eyes. I know what you've come back to do.

"A-fore I tell you, I want to say somethin' about Angel. You know, these Basques ain't a bad people; they're fightin'-men. In some ways they're right like the mountain-people yore daddy came from. Yore daddy's paw and me and the rest of us fit pretty hard for this country.

"When the Basques came pilin' in here we jumped 'em. We didn't allow to let 'em have this land after what we'd been through. Lord only knows what we'd a-done with it all! But they stuck; and they've done pretty well.

"Lookin' back, I see how foolish the whole fight was. But men go on like that—like Angel has done. He's been the biggest fool of all. Now, things has changed—everythin' but him! The country's changed; the Basques has changed; and they're goin' to keep on changin'. They can't do nuthin' else; they ain't ever going back to Spain.

"And so I want to ask you—what's Angel got for himself out of all the hatin' he's done? He's an old man—I reckon he's known his mistakes for a long time—but he's afeered to admit it now; he's too stiff-necked. I guess God's just lettin' him live till he's willin' to eat crow.

"No matter what you do to him, Joseph, I won't hold it ag'in you. He's got it a-comin' to him; but boy, if you'd only promise—"

"Please! Do not exact a promise from me. This matter concerns only that man and me. No one must come between us. But his death would only defeat my purpose. Angel Irosabal must live. Tell me—who killed Kit Dorr?"

The suddenness of the question made Peter

recoil. It grew very still in the little dug-out. Both man and boy seemed to be caught up and held motionless in a tensely charged way. Waiting—one to hear, and the other to voice—a brief syllable or two; and both fully conscious that the course of their lives might well be changed thereby.

Joseph's eyes never left the old man's. Seconds dragged by before Peter's lips moved. No sound escaped them, however, and when he did speak his voice was dry, unnatural.

"It—it—was—Andres."

"Andres—" It was a whisper.

For a seemingly endless time, the boy remained motionless, his eyes closed. Slippy-foot stared at him anxiously. She whimpered softly as Joseph sat down.

"Andres—my mother's brother!" he repeated. He did not raise his voice, but the hatred and bitterness with which he spoke gave his words a dreadful sound.

"It was Andres," Peter muttered, but his was not the air of one who enjoys his own tale. To escape the boy's staring eyes, he spread his blankets upon the floor and made ready for sleep, but as he bent over, the expected question came from the boy:

"How do you know?"

"Joseph," Peter scolded, "don't look at me that-a-way. You make me feel all clammy and cold as if death was stalkin' around in *here*."

"Oh, man, go on," the boy insisted. "How do you know it was Andres?"

The old man pulled off his boots and sat down upon his blankets before he spoke.

"I heard him say so," he began. "When I got into that pocket, I crawled way in below the ledge and rolled up and tried to go to sleep. I was on foot and thankin' my stars I didn't have no animal to look after that night, when I caught sound of some one comin' up the hogback. I don't remember who I thought it was. It wa'n't late—'bout eight thirty. A man had to yell that night to make himself heard.

"I savvy Basque pretty well, and the first word I made out was *zaldiak*—horses. In those days the Basque *gente* wa'n't particularly welcome round here. I got kinda curious right off. And the next minute I heard those horses comin' right down into that pocket. One of the men—they was two of them—tried to strike a light, but you couldn't make fire even thar that night." Peter paused and reflected for a moment.

"I didn't say nuthin'," he went cn; "I knew they didn't know I was there."

"Who was the second man?" Joseph interrupted.

"Andres's kid brother, Timoteo. The kid went on directly, but he left Andres in the pocket. Andres was to follow him on foot when he thought the time was right. Well, I was doin' some pretty fast thinkin'. Here was hell to pay, for fair, and me not knowin' what to do.

"I wa'n't afraid of Timoteo. I reckoned your daddy could manage him if this thing that was brewin' was aimed at your folks. Andres had me trapped; and so we stayed thar—me under the ledge and him backed against his horse— waitin' and waitin'.

"I guess an hour must have passed. God, it was awful. I wanted to yell and get out where they was air; I was stranglin'—Andres thar all that time, so close, and not knowin' that I was watchin' him.

"Well, he gave a yell all of a sudden and jumpin' into his saddle he fanned it out of thar, leadin' the kid's horse behind him. I got out and stretched myself directly. I hadn't been able to do no thinkin' with him thar.

"I'd heard them tossing a word back and forth that I hadn't savvied. It came to me, then— nippers! That meant wire! I began to see a thing or two right off. Those boys were out to cut the Circle-Z fence. Wa'n't no other wire for 'em to cut.

"I felt considerable relieved. Thad Taylor of the Circle-Z wa'n't no bosom friend of mine. 'Let him look out for his own wire,' I said to myself and I crawled back into my nest, thinkin' that those boys had a good night for what they was about, whether they got away with it or not.

"But I wa'n't any sleepier then than I am right now, which I ain't at all. I knew if they came back, I'd hear them. More than an hour passed; nuthin' happened. And then I heard horses comin' on the run. I got up and listened.

"In about a minute Andres flashed by. He was cryin'—mad! He was gibberin' to himself in Basque: 'I killed him! I killed him!' He had the kid's horse on a rope, but the saddle was empty.

" 'He's killed the kid,' I told myself, and so I thought until the posse dug me out and told me that Kit Dorr had been murdered, and that they was after your paw.

"Save for tellin' Kincaid, I ain't said nuthin' 'till now. You can guess what happened, can't you?—two men was killed that night."

"Dorr and Timoteo—"

"Ain't a doubt of it. The boy went down to cut the wire. Kit got him. Andres came along later, stampedin' your sheep. The kid must have crawled away and tipped him off, and Andres nailed Kit."

"A supposition—"

"Facts is what I'm tellin' you," Peter exclaimed. "Kit was killed by a .30-30 bullet. Andres had the rifle."

"But Timoteo—I remember it was said that he had gone to Spain."

Peter smiled weakly.

"So it was said," he replied. "But he's never come back. Timoteo went a lot further than Spain that night."

"But his body—?"

"Never been found—leastwise not that any one knows of. I looked for it. You know, Joseph," and Peter fastened his eyes on the boy's face, "I've always felt that your mother found it— that somewhere on this mountain little Timoteo lies buried. He was Angel's baby. I tell you he looked for him. You know how range is now— he needs more—but he's never run a head of stock up here. In his eyes this mountain is a tomb."

"Yes; and from this tomb I will arise to humble him and his sons."

He got to his feet and stood over the old man. Unconsciously he raised his right hand.

"When you leave here, make no mystery of me.

Let them know I am Joseph. You can serve me best that way. I have come back to avenge my mother; to see justice done my father—and it will be done unto both of them!"

The blazing wrath of the avenger flamed in his eyes.

"When I found my mother cold in death she held my school-boy slate clutched in her hands. On it she had written a message. I have come back to fulfill every word of it. I do not doubt that she found Timoteo, nor do I question but what I know where to find his body. He will serve me well.

"Angel Irosabal—he and his sons—shall be humbled, broken—cast into the dust. Let them look to me! For I warn you, my friend, that the seven lean years are upon this land, even as they were upon Egypt. The time of plenty has passed.

"There shall be no rain in summer; no snow in winter; the sage and grass shall wither and die, and a famine will be upon the land. The very men whose flocks have worn the roads to powder will live to see their sheep dying of hunger."

Peter stared at him as though he were a character that had stepped out of the Bible. He sucked in his breath noisily as he waited for the boy to go on.

"Never have they thought of the lean years,

and yet, it was the lean years that drove them out of California—and lack of food will drive them out of this valley. In its abundance, they have wasted this land and they will have no place to turn in their anguish. They will sell their flocks and herds for a pittance, or they will die."

Joseph lowered his hand and gazed intently at Peter.

"And now, my friend," he said, "a secret for a secret. There is one who has moved about in these hills—unknown, unseen—leasing land, contracting for it against a day to come. And that day is near. He has schemed well. For months he has known that when fall comes, a scratch of the pen will close the Reservation to sheep.

"And though he knows me not—that man is my father."

Old Peter was left speechless. There was something uncanny, unreal, about this boy. He spoke with such an air of finality, of truth, that the aged man felt the absurdity of questioning his words. Joseph's appearance, his dress and the weirdness of his surroundings combined to instill in him a feeling of awe such as no other man had ever awakened. A Basque, steeped in superstition, would run in fear from the boy.

Just now, with that matter-of-fact tone which one uses to announce trivial happenings, he made a statement not less startling than word of his own presence there on the mountain had been. And the calm assurance with which he looked forward to the adjusting of his account with his grandfather; his frankly expressed conviction that he was there as God's instrument; the biblical flavor of his speech—Peter thought of these things in a muddled way.

He wished himself elsewhere. As in a vision, he saw the Gaults—father and son—biding their time, waiting the propitious moment, gathering strength to strike—grim, unrelenting, unforgiving, never forgetting, placing their dependence on God. By comparison, he felt himself impotent, decisionless.

Was it fear of this boy that made him so uneasy? Hot anger flared in his old.veins as he answered his own question. Suddenly, he reached out for his boots, determined to sleep in the open, but his hand paused in mid-air. Some one was coming.

Peter cocked his head and listened expectantly. The sound which reached his ears was not that of a human footfall, nor was it the soft pad-pad of an animal's feet. It was strange, grating, harsh in the stillness.

Peter glanced at Slippy-foot. Her hair was

ruffled, and she was backing away from the door, but she neither whimpered nor growled.

Joseph had turned and was staring out into the night. Peter tried to read his feeling from the pose of his back, but he found it straight, untensed—apparently untouched by any emotion.

Whatever was approaching the dug-out was coming toward it with a measured stride. Peter had become aware of the rhythmic insistence of the ghastly sound. He felt a shiver pass up and down his spine.

It was not the wolf shiver. He had trembled at the timber-gray's call too many times not to recognize it. Never had the wolf-cry brought him a sense of fear, and he knew that the thing which gripped him now was fear.

He drew his legs up as he waited. Slippy-foot nudged closer to him, and he was glad she was there.

Then in the doorway appeared the thing that had frightened him. Blacker than the night it was; with lordly mien it strutted into the room, its black claws tapping upon the hard-packed floor, its gold-rimmed eyes wide, piercing—the wisdom of the world in their depths—a giant crow!

It made no cry as it advanced. Peter's mouth had sagged open. As in a daze, he stared at the sleek feathered thing standing before him. He drew back into his blankets, his blood cold. Watching, he saw the great bird spread its wings and rise to the table, where it perched in forbidding importance, its black head rolling from side to side—ominous, chilling, the hand-servant of Death.

For forty years this grisly bird had scoured the desert, despised of men and feasting on the dead, but doing that which nature had intended it to do; justifying its place in the great scheme of things that is life; its only law, the survival of the fittest. Ever had man's hand been raised against it. And yet it entered the dug-out this night, unafraid.

Peter wanted to cry out and ask what ill-omened business brought it there, but his voice would not come. Everything had a queer draw to it to-night! Where would this hellish nightmare end? He wanted to get out—away; to fill his lungs with clean air again. He willed his hands to grasp his boots, but they refused to obey, and he could only sit and stare at that great, black, blinking thing there before him.

"Look not on this bird as an enemy," he heard Joseph say. "He is an old friend—I call him Grimm. He passes on all that I do; and he is never wrong. He never mistakes an enemy for a friend. He it was who told me you were coming up the mountain to-night. He says nothing now because he accepts you as a friend."

"Take him away," Peter gasped. "He makes my flesh creep. Are you mad? Havin' such things about you!"

Joseph smiled at him.

"I understand you," he said. "Here you see me, clad in rags, my companions the scavenger coyote and the carrion crow—outcasts of the desert—reviled, unloved—what a picture! And yet it is given even unto the lowest to reward kindness with faith.

"When you speak of me, speak of my companions, for we are three; and if the least of these shall love me, I will not fail."

CHAPTER IX.

FROM the day that he had returned to Buckskin, Joseph had cast his eyes at its rocky crest. Throughout the years he had looked forward to the time when he should stand, there and read the message his mother had left him. In fancy, he had done so a thousand times. And yet—now that he was there—he had found himself reluctant to face it.

As he had grown older, a fixed idea of what he would find had settled on him; but his return to the mountain had destroyed that assurance. He had expected to find his old home still standing, and in his bitterness at finding it destroyed he had told himself he dared not hope that any sign remained for him on Buckskin.

Peter Organ had explained many things to Joseph. For a day after the old man had left, the boy did not leave the coulee. With great patience he arranged in his mind what Peter had said. Of one thing he was certain—his mother's message was a secret no longer. He felt that he knew its contents in full. It was not what he had expected. But his way was clear before him now; and at sunrise, the following morning, he stood upon the mountain-top.

The world was still—hushed with the wonder of the coming day. Far below him, the desert floated in a lavender sea; to the east the distant Tuscarora Mountains were splashed with warm yellows and cold pinks.

Slippy-foot leaped to the topmost pinnacle and, lifting her head, she barked a greeting to the Thing of Light. The sun leaped clear of the far horizon and flooded mountain and plain with its vibrant rays. As if pursued, the gray shadows, lingering in cañon and draw, took to flight and were gone.

At this moment the glory of the universe was God's. Joseph raised his hands devoutly and lifting his eyes to Heaven, he gave thanks to his Creator.

How long he stood there or how many minutes passed before he realized that he was staring at a message carved on the enduring granite of the pinnacle upon which Slippy-foot stood, he could not have said. Slowly his brain began to function. His eyes grew wide, for the message they read was for him. Word by word, he said it aloud.

SACRED
To the Memory of
JOSEPH GAULT

The letters were uneven, graceless—carved upon the naked rock by his mother's feeble hands. Pride, love of her who had loved his father so well, consumed him. In comparison, all else seemed small and mean.

It was not his way to fall upon his knees in humility. Erect, militant, he addressed himself to his Maker—"talking to God," as he would have said—and it well may be that Buckskin shall never again hear such a prayer.

In the end, his eyes sought the message once more—the lasting tribute of a woman's faith. He came close to it and touched the letters with his fingers. Although his eyes were dry, his lips were white as he turned away. Memories of his boyhood rushed to his mind, and with the haunting freshness with which one sees things in a dream, he saw himself a lad again.

Solemn-visaged Grimm came and perched beside him, his red-lidded, gold-rimmed eyes blinking questioningly; but Joseph gave no sign that he saw him. The boy had waited so long for this hour on the mountain-top that he was in no great hurry to bring his wandering thoughts back to the task of searching for the secret which he knew

must be hidden there. When he did begin searching for it, he arose leisurely, his face almost
devoid of any sign of eagerness.

In a tiny fissure directly beneath the inscription,
he found a heap of small rocks. Something about
the way in which they were piled seemed to say
that human hands had once arranged them in a
more exact formation. Indians often covered the
graves of their dead with such cairns. Was this,
then, the secret his mother had left him—
Timoteo's grave?

Joseph bent down and began removing the rocks
nearest the inscription. He had not gone far before he saw the neck of a bottle protruding from
the cairn. Grimm cawed as Joseph grasped it.

The boy glanced at him apprehensively. From
where he perched, the great bird could not have
seen the bottle. It contained a paper—a letter!

Joseph shook his head as he broke off the neck
of the bottle, believing, but far from understanding how Grimm had known that the quest was
ended.

On drawing forth the letter, Joseph discovered
a second message, in Basque, pinned to it. This
second letter of only a few lines had been written
with a pencil upon a leaf of paper torn from
a note-book. The other letter was addressed to
him. It read:

My Joseph:

My brother Timoteo lies here. Dorr shot him. I found his body and buried it. In his hand was the message you will find pinned to this letter.

It will tell you what you want to know. Your father was an innocent man. You must see that justice is done him. Think not of my people. If they suffer, so it must be, for your great duty is to yourself and to the man whose name you bear.

Above all else, my son, be true to yourself. It is my great wish.

Joseph exhibited no surprise at what he read, for old Peter had prepared him for this very thing. Timoteo's message, however, was of absorbing interest. He studied it with puzzled brow, raking his mind for a word of two out of the past. Except for three or four simple expressions, he knew no Basque. The message was addressed to Angel. Joseph made out part of the first line. It began:

My brother, Andres——

Several lines lower, he caught Dorr's name. Allowing for the contractions of the language and the combinations of words which could be expressed by one word, he took it for granted that whatever the first line said about "My brother Andres" it had no reference to Dorr.

Andres's name was repeated in the line in which Dorr's name occurred. So the message must say two things: something about Andres and Dorr; and something about Andres and Timoteo. Joseph could only guess what the latter statement might be. And yet, it was vital to his plans that he know for a certainty what this message said.

He wished that Peter had not gone on. He was one of the few, outside of the Basques themselves, who even attempted to speak the tongue. Later, Joseph realized that it was unlikely that the old man could read or write a word of Basque, for his knowledge of the language was doubtless restricted to a matter of sounds.

During the succeeding days, the boy sat for hours with Timoteo's message in his hands. In all that time, he deciphered only one phrase: *"d-arrai-t"*—"It follows me."

There was a ranger's cabin just beyond Coal Creek. Joseph thought of going there in the hope of meeting some of the Basque herders then in the Reserve. He soon argued himself out of the notion, however, for if Timoteo's message said that Andres had killed Dorr, then no one but old Angel himself must read it. It was, potentially, a powerful weapon, and not to be misused.

For five days after Peter had left the mountain, Joseph did nothing but study the letter. No one came to spy on him, for Peter talked but little in town and that little was received skeptically.

Men laughed at his story of the lean years to come.

Joseph had convinced Peter that night in the dug-out, but even he found the tale fanciful now that he was back in his accustomed haunts. At times he wondered if the boy had not been touched by some strange malady of the brain. If he could have seen Joseph staring trance-like at the penciled note for hours at a time, Slippy-foot and Grimm at his feet, apparently as sorely perplexed as their master, he would have found it hard to have believed otherwise.

The deciphering of Timoteo's message had become an obsession. Just where it might have carried Joseph, it is impossible to say, but he was destined to have the note made plain to him in a most startling manner.

After reading his mother's letter, he had replaced it in the bottle and brought it to the dug-out. Timoteo's note had so engaged his attention ever since that he had not touched the bottle. That he picked it up now was only because he was about to pin the two messages together again preparatory to putting them away. He had determined to go back to the mountain-top and search the cairn for some sign of the missing note-book.

Idly turning over his mother's letter, as he pinned the two papers together, he was rendered speechless at finding himself gazing at a translation of Timoteo's note. Perspiration dewed his brow as he stared at it. It was addressed to Timoteo's father, and said:

My brother Andres, the coward, has left me to die. I called to him, but he took the horses and ran. Dorr shot me as I finished cutting the fence. Andres killed him as he bent over me. But I see now that he will hang for it. It is morning. I hear a crow. It follows me. It has not long to wait. Grieve not, my father. What were you to expect of men who were raised to hate their own?

TIMOTEO.

Grimm cawed as Joseph finished reading the note. The boy looked at him coldly.

"Grimm," he muttered, "I wonder if it was you who followed Timoteo and cawed a requiem for his soul. And you, Slippy-foot—what would you have to say if you could speak? For once the eyes of both of you are veiled. But no matter. We have waited long enough. To-night the three of us shall attend one whose debt is heavy."

CHAPTER X.

THE SYMBOL OF HELPLESSNESS.

ALMOST a week had passed since Joseph had left the coulee, and in that time, although his flock numbered only a score, the sweet grass had been grazed to the roots. So having made up his mind to go to the valley that night, he moved across the mountain in the early afternoon, driving his sheep to the timber-clover above the spring.

One would hardly have guessed from his placid face that the long-awaited fight was so near at hand. His present position afforded him even a better view of the valley than was to be had from the coulee, and leaning on his staff, he stood for many minutes gazing moodily at old Angel's *caserio*, a dazzling white in the afternoon sunlight.

It pleased him to know that he would find his grandfather alone. Not for another two weeks would Angel's sons or grandsons return from the Reserve for supplies. Joseph thought of the time when he had been turned away from the great man's door without even a sight of him.

It should be different this night. And yet, he deliberately kept himself from forming any definite plan of what he must do. This meeting to-night must be free to proceed as fate willed. At best, it could be but the beginning of his grandfather's retribution.

It may have been fancy, but Joseph felt that Grimm and Slippy-foot caught his mood. Both were plainly nervous, and when he gave the word to start back down the mountain they obeyed eagerly.

The sun had dropped below the horizon by the time Joseph reached the coulee, and while Slippy-foot worked the flock until it was ready to bed down, Joseph cooked his supper. A peculiar sadness rested upon his face now. To his ears came the sounds he had always associated with evening —the calling of the whippoorwill, the cheeping of the plover in the sage and, from some distant peak, the barking of a coyote. Unconsciously he threw back his head and gazed up at the crest of Buckskin.

He found it as he had ever found it at this hour—majestic in its rose-colored mantle, the gift of the sun which he could no longer see. Already the valley was bathed in opalescent twilight. So vividly did these sights and sounds bring back the past that he turned and gazed across the coulee at the spot where the cabin had once stood. All that was needed to complete the picture was his old home, a wisp of smoke curling lazily up from its wide chimney. Here he had stood a hundred times and more at this hour, the appetizing aroma of supper in his nostrils.

So poignant were his memories that he winced. . . . All these years! He wet his lips with his tongue as he stared about him in the deepening twilight. Soon night fell and the valley faded from view. The time to go had arrived. Without invitation, Grimm fluttered to his shoulder. Slippy-foot needed no word and she slunk away.

Joseph chose to follow the old trail which led into the valley by way of the Circle-Z fence— now just a fence, and no longer the barrier it once had been, for the West had changed. The boy communed with himself as he went along. The night had its effect on him, and his thoughts were grim.

In the days since he had roamed the mountain as a boy, old Thad Taylor, the owner of the Circle-Z, had built a new ranch-house at the mouth of the box cañon in which Eagan and Tiny Mears had weathered the great storm. Joseph caught the glow of its lighted windows as he reached the fence. He had known of it, and he went on without halting. Some minutes later the moon peeked over the shoulder of the mountain and bathed the valley with its mellow light.

Before long, Joseph came to an arroyo through which a well-worn trail led to Angel Irosabal's *caserio*. He turned into it, but he had proceeded only a little way when he saw Slippy-foot pause and raise her nose. He stopped short, and the bleating of a lamb reached his ears. It was off to his right in the tumbled *malpais*.

He started on, but the lamb bleated again. It was a pitiable cry, hopeless and entreating, and so out of key with his thoughts that Joseph trembled as he called Slippy-foot back and started across the arroyo in the direction from which the lamb had called.

Five minutes later Slippy-foot announced that she had found the lamb. The coyote's presence filled it with fear, and it bleated loudly until Joseph reached it. He saw that the lamb had stepped into an old, rusted coyote-trap. Using his staff as a pry, he opened the trap and picked up the lamb. Its right foreleg was torn, and it began to swell rapidly.

Joseph looked at the lamb wonderingly, seeing in it the symbol of helplessness and, as such, at variance with the spirit which motivated him this night. The lamb raised its head and with eyes heavy with suffering, gazed at him questioningly.

Suddenly, Joseph saw himself mean—the business he was about less vital, less urgent than it had been.

Slippy-foot had gone on and she turned and eyed Joseph sullenly as she saw that he made no move to follow her. Grimm fluttered his wings as if impatient.

Joseph shook his head as he sensed their urging. To leave the lamb here was to let it die. He was quite aware of the tragedies that befall stock running wild on the range, and in a way he was hardened to it, recognizing it as inevitable. Nevertheless, he could not go on.

The Circle-Z ranch house was no great distance away, and although old Thad Taylor was reputed to have never overcome his hatred of sheep and all that sheepmen stood for, Joseph decided to take the stricken lamb to him.

Slippy-foot still stood her distance and she came back grudgingly when Joseph called to her. He smiled as he glanced from her to Grimm and found the crow shaking his head solemnly as if decrying this move.

"No—," he said banteringly; "you cannot tempt me. We are going back. And if this lamb had half the wisdom of either of you, he would smile with me for, beyond doubt, he belongs to Angel Irosabal."

CHAPTER XI.

THE SEED IS PLANTED.

SOME there were who had smiled when Angel Irosabal had first sown wheat in Paradise Valley, but in those days water-rights were not so jealously guarded, and he had irrigated his fields to suit his pleasure. Martin Creek came tumbling out of the Santa Rosas on his range, and with much ado, especially in early spring, cut across his ranch to the Circle-Z line.

To help himself to its bounty was quite in keeping with the code of practice of those early days. It followed, therefore, that his wheat thrived. With passing years he had given more and more acreage to it, for he was shrewd enough to see that it was more profitable to send his flocks into the Reserve than to graze them on land which could be sown to crops.

Other men followed his lead. Water-rights became of vital importance, bringing a mass of litigation which still clogs the courts of Nevada. Wheat became an item of importance in the life of the Valley and, with the thriftiness of the

Basque, Angel had built a mill in which to grind the golden harvest. At best, it was a crude affair which the valley soon outgrew, but the old Basque did not hurry to replace it with a larger and better. mill, for it was like him to have his investment guaranteed before making it.

A new mill would need more water. To make the mill profitable, the valley must produce a larger crop, and only more water could make that possible. And from where was this water to come? Martin Creek was the one unfailing source of supply, and from the Santa Rosas to the Little Humboldt every man with a water-right was either using or selling the maximum number of inches allowed him by law. So Angel saw his mill standing idle if in the future some other crop should prove more profitable, for it would claim part of the water now being used in the irrigation of wheat.

Not only to guard against this, but to make some alliance that would guarantee him an even larger sowing, became his chief concern and for three months he had pursued it. Next to himself, the Circle-Z claimed the greatest number of inches. Taylor had leased his water rights in Martin Creek to Paradise ranchers, depending on the North Fork for his own supply.

And now a strange thing happened, for although it was popularly supposed that Thad Taylor would have nothing to do with a sheepman, and a Basque in particular, he and Angel pooled their interests in Martin Creek. For although Thad's hatred of the Basque was long-lived, it in no way matched his love of the dollar, and it seemed certain that the arrangement he had made with Angel would line his pockets. That the thing they proposed doing was unfair, and less than honorable, mattered not at all to either.

The men who had been leasing Thad's water were dependent on it. Whatever value was placed on their ranches was contingent on their being able to renew their leases. A ranch without water is about as worthless a thing as Nevada can boast.

Thad and Angel were well aware of this, and it was their intention to buy in these properties at their own figure, to put what they could of them to wheat and to divide the profits. It was this very business which had taken Angel to the Circle-Z this day, and as Joseph with the wounded lamb in his arms started back to Thad Taylor's ranch-house, Angel and Thad lingered over their supper.

Little Billy, in his day a round-up cook of some renown and now Thad's chef and man-at-arms in general, was bent on clearing the table. He slipped in whenever it seemed propitious and retrieved a dish or platter. Thad soon discouraged him, however, for he was an autocratic, overbearing old man steeped in having his own way.

With more tact it is true, the old rancher had dismissed his granddaughter, for of all the creatures who trod the earth, Thad Taylor loved and feared none as he did Necia. Moreover, he knew that the business he was discussing with Angel would not pass muster in her eyes.

When they had finished their scheming, Thad called her in. She was beautiful in a spiritual sense, her young body—she was only twenty—without hint of voluptuousness. As she stood in the doorway, her head lightly poised, it seemed incredible that the day would ever come when the purely physical loveliness of her would dim the ethereal beauty that was hers now. Angel glanced at her as if expecting some bird-like note to issue from her slightly parted lips.

Necia waited, however, for her grandfather to speak, and as he gathered up his papers, she glanced from him to Angel, appraising each in her own way, wondering what they had in common. The two men were of about the same age and shrewdness was written upon the face of each, but in no other way were they even remotely alike, for her grandfather was short, heavy—bald; his ruddy cheeks and rounded nose almost giving the lie to his severe, tight-lipped mouth. Angel was tall, cadaverous, angular, a great shock of iron-gray hair cascading over his high forehead.

Necia had heard him reviled many times, but in the four or five visits he had made to the Circle-Z she had found him courteous and patient. She had been raised, however, in a household where the Basque had been held no better than a Mexican—her mother, old Thad's daughter, had shared this view—and Necia found it difficult to overcome the prejudice.

Thad glanced at her apprehensively as he straightened up, for he had felt her scrutiny.

"Well, well, Necia," he exclaimed brusquely, as was his habit when trying to cover up, "I can tell you a secret now: we're goin' to have a real flour-mill."

Necia smiled. "Meaning that some one has lost his water rights, eh?" she queried provokingly.

"Never you mind about that," Thad grinned. "Business is business. I'm no organized charity. Go on and play those new records for us, will you?"

Necia shook her head as she glanced at the wax rolls—in that day quite the last word in talking-machine records.

"They are *terrible*, grandfather," she said teasingly. "—'The Bull Frog and the Coon'—'Flanigan's Wake'—" Necia made a wry face as she read the labels aloud.

"Terrible?" Thad snorted. "'Flanigan's Wake?' Why, when I was a young buck they wa'n't no better tune a-goin' than that! But that's young-folks for you!" he went on vehemently, pretending an anger he was far from feeling. "Old-time things ain't good enough for them no more."

"Maybe, that is best, eh *señor?*" Angel argued.

This was unexpected. Thad whirled on him in fine dudgeon.

"You a-goin' to take sides ag'in me, too?" he gasped. "Necia don't need no help. She bosses me to death now. I tell you, young-folks has got too much imagination. They've got things all figured out in advance. Makes me feel obsolete."

"Oh, poor grandfather," Necia said mockingly as she perched herself upon the arm of his chair.

"See?" Thad protested. "The tyranny of the female—it's awful. You can't make them take you seriously. If you don't agree with them, they laugh at you. Why, for three weeks she's been tryin' to make believe there's a ragged, half starved, no good—"

"I did not say he was a no-good," Necia objected.

"No, you didn't.   But if there was such a person, what else could he be—hidin' out on a mountain, goin' around without shoes, hair down his back—playin' around with a handful of crippled sheep that he's picked up, God knows where! Bah!   Do you think I'm mad?"

"Oh, so you've heard those tales, too, *señor?*" Angel inquired.

"Hain't heard nothin' else!" Thad exclaimed. "My boys don't talk about anythin' else.   They say he's got a coyote herdin' his flock!   D'you ever hear anythin' so downright foolish? Grown-up men ought to know better.   If they're out at night and a coyote shuts up all of a sudden or a bob-cat quits his squawlin', they nudge each other and mutter, 'Joseph!'   It makes me sick."

"And the crow, grandfather," Necia said tauntingly; "don't forget it."

"That's beyond me, that crow stuff," Thad declared helplessly.   "I ain't even goin' to repeat that."

Necia smiled, but Angel's eyes were mirthless.

"My friend," he said after a moment's hesitation, "the tales you scoff at are true—even the crow."

"What?" Thad brought his chair down with a thud.   Angel nodded.

"They are true," he repeated.

There was a convincing quality in the old Basque's voice. Thad knew he had heard the truth, and his mouth sagged as he stared speechlessly at the old Basque. Necia was less surprised, but her face grew sober as she and her grandfather waited for Angel to speak.

"He has been living on the mountain for months," their visitor went on after some deliberation.

"Have you seen him?" Thad demanded.

"I have seen his fires at night. One of my young men has seen him."

Thad whistled softly. "So that is why your boys went around by way of the spring, eh?"

"That is why, *señor*," Angel answered, somewhat disconcerted. "You know Peter Organ— he has talked with this man."

"What did he have to say?"

Angel scowled and got up and reached for his hat. Suddenly turning and confronting Necia and her grandfather, he exclaimed excitedly:

"He threatens us with famine! He says our crops will fail, our herds die for want of water!' *Mal rayo la parta!* (May an evil stroke of lightning smother him.) He says that the seven lean years are upon this valley as they were upon Egypt!"

Thad laughed loudly at this.

"The seven lean years, eh?" he queried sarcastically. "I guess you and me know that there's been lean years right along for those who look for them. Year in and year out we been here. We ain't done so bad. I reckon we'll git by. Lean years for lean heads! Quotin' the Bible to Peter, eh? I might a-known he was a religion-struck fool."

"Well—do you condemn him for warning you?" Necia asked.

"*Condemn* him?" Thad questioned. "Humph! What a fool?"

Angel was standing at the window, staring out into the soft night.

"But, *señor*," he murmured without turning, "this is the last day of May. It has not rained this month."

"Just a dry spring," Thad retorted. "You don't mean to tell me you take any stock in this wild talk?"

"It's strange—strange," Angel answered as much to himself as to Thad and Necia.

"Well, it's your land he's on," said Thad. "I wouldn't stand no foolishness from him. I'd make him git. You—you ain't *afraid* of him?"

Angel shook his head slowly.

"Joseph," he muttered only half aloud. "—

Joseph! It spells power. *Jaincoa!* I hate that name."

Thad nodded, and patted Necia's hand.

"So do I," he said slowly. "I haven't forgotten. Why, I—I—" and as he paused to find a word he heard something scratching at the door. And as all three of them stared, the door opened and Slippy-foot stalked into the room.

Thad's eyes bulged. The coyote stopped and looked from one to the other of them. Angel, at the window, had thrown up his hand as if to ward off something evil, and he stood seemingly petrified, fear written upon his face. Even Necia trembled and drew back. Though no one of them had ever seen Slippy-foot before, the manner of her entrance chilled their blood.

CHAPTER XII.

NECIA.

A COYOTE walking into a ranch-house! Only a rangeman can appreciate their surprise. Before they had recovered, the weird tap, tap, of something crossing the gravel outside the door reached their ears. The next instant, Grimm, black and sleek, strutted into the room with the mien of an archbishop.

Necia heard Angel gasp as he caught his breath. Her grandfather was having an equally hard time of it. Their apparent helplessness steadied rather than alarmed Necia, and she threw back her head and bravely faced Grimm and Slippy-foot.

Grimm blinked his great gold-rimmed eyes as he surveyed the room and its occupants, and the wisdom and shrewdness that shone in them seemed to mock the petty schemes and secrets of the men before him. Crossing to where Angel stood, he humped his wings and looking up at the Basque, he deliberately clacked his tongue, and the sound was not unlike a laugh. Angel winced, feeling that the great bird was peering into his very soul. Grimm continued to regard him solemnly for another three or four seconds. Turning, then, he hopped upon the table.

A bread crust caught his wandering gaze, and tearing it into bits, he ate it with relish; but, even as he ate, his eyes roamed continually from Angel to Thad. He had been in the room fully a minute, and in that time no one had spoken. Necia could not but wonder why he never glanced at her, and she could not repress a start when, without warning, he raised his wings and hopped upon her shoulder. At that instant a voice called:

"Grimm!"

The crow cawed audaciously and sailed to the floor, and as he did so Joseph reached the doorway. For some minutes they had known he must come, and although Grimm and Slippy-foot had prepared them for his arrival, they could not take their eyes off him as he stood framed against the night, the wounded lamb in his arms. The lamp's mellow light glinted against his tanned cheeks and accentuated the luster of his eyes.

A majestic dignity rested upon him as he glanced at each of them in turn. Necia felt it. The serenity which cloaked him made light of his ragged clothes, and the girl, urged by an impulse she little understood, took a step toward him. She would have spoken had not her grandfather recovered his tongue and, brushing her aside, cried out angrily:

"State your business!"

Joseph's face retained its placidity. A moment before he had recognized Angel, and though his surprise had been great at finding him here, he had not betrayed it. He properly supposed that the man who addressed him was Thad Taylor and knowing him to be, by reputation, an irascible old man, it pleased Joseph to answer him at his own pleasure.

"I have come to you for help," he said.

"Help?" Thad shouted. "Git that truck out of my house!" he raged, pointing to Slippy-foot and Grimm.

Joseph looked at Angel as if asking him if he concurred in this, and the expression on the old Basque's face well repaid the boy. Necia thought she saw his eyes smile as he motioned to the coyote.

"Go," he murmured.

Slippy-foot hesitated for a moment and bared her fangs as she glared at Angel. Joseph lifted his hand then, and she slunk out.

"And you, Grimm," he said to the crow.

Grimm clacked his tongue sarcastically and, swaying from side to side, pattered across the floor and was gone.

Thad's sigh was one of relief.

"What's the meanin' of this?" he cried, and his voice sounded natural once more. "What do you want me to do for you?"

"For me—nothing. This lamb is suffering. I took it out of a trap a short while ago. Its leg is torn—it needs attention."

"Don't bring no sheep to me," Thad answered wrathfully, oblivious to Angel's presence. "I reckon that ain't the first lamb that's stepped into a trap."

"No, unfortunately; but we know about this one. This poor, stricken thing—the most helpless of all God's creatures—can not ask you for aid. I do that. And you—will not—refuse me."

"You ain't got nuthin' else to do but run around gathering up crippled sheep, eh?" Thad asked insolently. "I hear you got most of your flock that-a-way. Why don't you take this one?"

"Because I believe it belongs to this man," and Joseph pointed to Angel. "I found it in the long arroyo below your fence."

Angel muttered something in Basque, but he did not offer to take the lamb. Joseph gazed at him and saw that he trembled as if palsied.

"What—what is your business?' Angel asked with some hesitation.

"I am a shepherd," Joseph answered.

"Shepherd, eh?—a herder," growled Thad.

"And your range?" Angel insisted.

"Wherever I find it."

The Basque nodded to himself.

"Do you want work?" he asked.

Joseph shook his head. "I have my work," he said slowly. "It is far from finished."

"Seven years of it yet, eh?" Thad questioned scornfully. "Seven lean years!—Huh!"

"They will come to pass!" Joseph declared with some heat.

"You can't preach religion to me," Thad shot back.

"I have no religion to preach," Joseph asserted, "and if I seem to have, it is more than I intend. I ask only that men do unto me as I do unto them. And meanwhile, this lamb suffers."

"I guess if you go around to the bunk-house some of the boys will fix you up," Thad said by way of compromise. The coyote—the crow—the boy's quiet confidence—his unwavering eyes—had combined to put a bit of fear into Thad's heart.

Necia had taken no part in the conversation, and as her grandfather had stormed at Joseph she had retreated to the other side of the table. But her eyes had not left Joseph's face, and she came forward now on hearing him dismissed.

"Why, grandfather," she said disapprovingly, and Thad raised his eyebrows inquiringly; "we cannot send this man out, looking for help from our men. I don't know of any one who would have troubled about the lamb. I—I think it was noble of him to bother with it. I want him to come in."

For a moment Thad looked at her as if not comprehending what she had said. He was anxious to see Joseph gone.

"You orderin' me to do that?" he asked, his voice harsh.

"I ask it, grandfather," Necia said simply. "This is your home, and we cannot serve it better than by proving that a stranger can find justice and gratefulness here."

Thad nodded a grudging consent as Necia paused. Then facing Joseph, she said:

"Will you come in? I will take care of the lamb. I am Necia Dorr."

It was Joseph's turn to fall back. His eyes widened as he gazed at her—so militant—so unafraid. But his was not a feeling of fear. It was more a sense of reverential awe which swept over him and robbed him of the power to take his eyes away from her. So a humble peasant might have stood before Jeanne d'Arc.

Thad and Angel caught the look in the boy's

eyes, and they glanced at each other furtively. As they stared at him, they saw Joseph's eyes cloud.

"Necia Dorr?" he muttered to himself.

Dorr —! Kit Dorr — Necia Dorr — the Circle-Z! Could he doubt but what this beautiful girl, with her tumbled blonde hair, was Kit Dorr's daughter? Why it should matter so much he did not know, but his throat went dry at the thought and with his senses fogged, he heard Necia say:

"If you will carry the lamb into the kitchen, I will dress its leg."

Thad and Angel got up and watched him as he followed Necia out of the room. A curse escaped Thad's lips as he sank back into his chair. Angel still stood staring at the door through which Joseph had disappeared. He muttered something to himself and going to the table, he bent over and whispered in Thad's ear:

"Do you know who he is?"

Angel's voice was as cold as death and it and the look in his eyes made Thad pop erect as if he were a jack-in-the-box.

"Who?" he demanded.

Angel straightened up, his eyes holding Thad's.

"That," he said at last, nodding toward the kitchen, "is Joe Gault's boy."

CHAPTER XIII.

"VENGEANCE IS MINE."

JOSEPH stood by silently as Necia cut away the wool from the lamb's torn leg; and save for holding the lamb while she washed the wound with a disinfectant, he found nothing he could do to help her. In a few minutes she had the injured leg bandaged. Joseph's desire for speech had never been greater, but a strange reticence gripped him, and now as Necia looked up at him, he could only ask her to allow him to put the lamb in Angel's rig which stood hitched outside.

"I think you have done enough already," Necia declared. "It was a fine thing to do. No wonder wild animals follow you around. I think I know why. But—have you had anything to eat?"

Joseph nodded and answered briefly:

"Before I left the mountain."

"It is a long way for one afoot. If you are going up the mountain yet to-night, I will loan you a horse."

"No—I will walk," Joseph replied uneasily, at a loss for words with which to express his gratitude for her thoughtfulness. "It is late—I will put the lamb in the rig—it is little enough to do—and go."

He was ill at ease, and he wondered if she suspected as much. He had no desire to end this moment with her, but he realized he had done no less, for Necia raised her eyebrows inquiringly, and picking up the lamb, handed it to him.

"It *is* getting late," she said softly.

There was nothing further to keep Joseph now, and he started to turn away, his eyes solemn. He paused as Necia said:

"If you—should ever come to the Circle-Z again, grandfather will treat you differently. He —is not heartless." A roguish twinkle came into her eyes as she hesitated momentarily. "I—I hope you will not find it too far to come again," she finished.

The fragrance of her hair swept into Joseph's nostrils as she opened the door for him. It was clean, invigorating, not unlike the perfume of young balsams in early spring. It shook him, and harking back to the speech of his boyhood, he said simply:

"I reckon I could find my way."

His sincerity and his use of the homely expression made Necia smile tenderly.

"You *reckon* you could, eh?" she trilled.

Both were young and keenly alive, and they laughed softly together.

"You are—a stranger," Necia said prettily. You—might give me your name—"

Joseph found her very alluring as her eyes dared him to answer while he hesitated, torn between the desire to tell her and the fear of cutting himself off from her forever if he did. To tell her that his father had not killed hers would be only to invite questions—to prove his statement —and the time for that was not yet. And then, wisdom whispered to him that this girl must find out the truth for herself. So he said only:

"Joseph."

"Just—Joseph?" Necia whispered.

He did not reply, nor did he catch the wistful light that crept into her eyes. He knew she was waiting for him to answer, and he nodded his head unhappily.

"Just—Joseph," he said, repeating her words, and his voice was strange to his own ears.

"That sounds very mysterious," she went on after a moment; "almost as if—as if it explained your presence in Nevada."

"You mean that I withhold my name from you because there is a blot on it?" Joseph asked, misunderstanding Necia's inference.

"No—no; not that," she hastened to answer.

She felt his eyes searching her own, and she colored as she struggled for words with which to express her thought. She stiffened as the boy said flatly:

"But that *is* my reason."

Necia stared at Joseph, wonderingly. She shook her head at last and smiled faintly.

"An injustice—a wrong! Something you are going to avenge—" she murmured, and then:

"I think that is exactly what I meant—not that you had come here to hide."

Joseph glanced at her shrewdly.

"Why—why do you think that?" he asked.

"I sensed it the moment you came in. Your speech is strange; you are hardly one of us—and yet, as you faced the Basque, I saw revenge flash in your eyes for a brief second. Your face was cruel. I even thought he cowered. He is a powerful man; and he has made many enemies."

Thoroughly disturbed by Necia's train of thought, the boy turned away, his eyes veiled.

"See—your face is hard now," she murmured. "I have guessed the truth."

Joseph did not reply. Unconsciously, Necia placed her hand upon his arm.

"Does it mean so much to you?" she asked.

"Everything," Joseph nodded quietly.

"I might have known you would say that. I

am sorry—truly. Revenge is so hopeless. It can bring you no happiness."

Her voice suddenly sounded sad. Joseph glanced up quickly, but Necia was looking beyond him at the great moon floating so lazily above the dim crest of distant Buckskin.

"You say that very positively," he said.

Necia nodded.

"My own life has proved it," she murmured, her voice trailing off into a whisper. "My grandfather never forgets or forgives a wrong. From childhood I seem to see him as always having been bent on righting the wrongs men had done him. He has never quite caught up with his revenge. I wonder, sometimes, if he realizes that he has no friends. Hardly any one comes here. It is very lonely—I feel it. We are never asked about. Men say that no one has ever got the best of grandfather—I wonder what else they say of him." Necia's thoughts wandered for a moment.

"If he had only forgiven one or two," she went on, "he would have had friends to-day. He needs them. But he'll not change. That you find a Basque in his home, after all his years of hating them, does not mean that he has changed. Angel Irosabal brings him a profit. Grandfather has sworn his life to hating sheep and sheepmen—the

Basques in particular—and he will go to his grave dreaming of avenging some wrong they did him. And yet, to my knowledge, it has been twelve years since a herder has infringed on him. My own father was killed in a fence-fight—a victim of this very spirit of revenge."

"Your father—Kit Dorr?" asked Joseph.

Necia's eyes came back to the boy.

"You knew him?' she questioned.

"I have heard men speak his name. You bear no malice toward the man who shot him?"

"I don't know. I suppose, even after all these years, that the sight of him would fill my heart with hatred. But I would try to forgive him. But I haven't kept him before me—I haven't thought about him. And I guess that sums up just what I am trying to say to you—that it is an affront to God to brood over an injustice, to keep it ever before you—alive and growing until you become its slave."

Necia's voice had risen, and she stopped, surprised at herself.

"I hadn't meant to say quite that," she said humbly. "Forgive me."

But Joseph had been deeply stirred, and he gave no sign that he heard her now.

"I have tried to keep hatred out of my heart!" he exclaimed earnestly. "For the dead cannot be avenged through hate. But I *have* come back to right a great wrong, and I will not be turned aside. I ask only justice. That will I have."

"But justice that demands an eye for an eye is often less than justice."

"And yet, I shall demand no less." His voice was determined, almost sullen in its intensity. "At this moment, I hold the lives and happiness of those who have wronged me and mine in my hand. I can crush them as you would crush an egg-shell. As easily as that!"

Joseph put out his hand, and Necia held her breath as she watched his fingers close until the nails sank into his flesh.

"And still—I have yet to raise my hand against any man. 'Vengeance is mine,' the Lord has said, and I do not intend to presume with Him. But if I do—if because I see in myself the messenger of His will—I will fail. Beyond all else, I am true to myself. No one can alter my purpose. Whenever opportunity has offered, I have never failed to do a man a favor. I have given all, and asked nothing."

"And already you have your reward," Necia declared. "Men who scoffed at you now respect you. You have made friends, whether you know it or not. You could do the people of this valley a wonderful service."

"I have," Joseph answered simply. "I have warned them. But they have not listened, even though the signs are everywhere. Not in fifty years has this valley been without water, so they see in me only a fanatic—a preacher of religion, your grandfather called me."

"But grandfather respects you. He does not know that he does, but—he does. When you spoke to him, he knew that he heard the truth. There—he is calling me—you will come again?"

"I may—have to," Joseph murmured with peculiar emphasis. Necia glanced at him questioningly.

"Have to?" she queried.

Joseph nodded.

"Your grandfather has never recalled the reward he offered for the capture of the man who killed your father. I may decide to claim it."

Necia drew back in surprise.

"You know where to find him?" she asked eagerly.

"He has never been away. He is not the man you suspect.

Thad had been standing beside Angel's buggy, waiting, and he started toward the side door now to find out what kept Necia. She heard him approaching, and she put her hand upon Joseph's arm again, touching him lightly.

"Tell me his name," she demanded. Her voice trembled.

"Not to-night," Joseph answered. "He is a brute and a bully—a coward. He shot your father in the back."

Necia's eyes flamed as Joseph spoke. Her face was as stern as his own, now.

"If I reveal his identity," he went on, "it will cost him his life. You think it over. If you can tell me, when you see me again, that you forgive him—that you do not demand that he pay for what he has done—I will give you his name."

Horror crept into Necia's eyes as she realized what he proposed.

"I understand you perfectly," she flared back. "You ask me to prove myself wrong—you make it very, very hard for me."

Her tone stabbed Joseph and he was about to speak when her grandfather reached the door.

"He's got a long drive ahead of him," Thad said petulantly, indicating Angel. "Let him get started."

Together they walked to the rig, and Joseph placed the lamb in it. The light streaming through the open door revealed Slippy-foot, the coyote, and Grimm, the crow, standing side by side, an oddly assorted pair of sentinels, so still that it was hard to believe they lived.

Necia glanced at them and saw their eyes shine as the light struck them. The crow was rolling his sinister orbs, alive to every movement of those before him. She tried to turn away, but Grimm held her fascinated. He looked for all the world like some high executioner come, not only to judge, but to punish those who were offensive to him.

She caught her breath as she felt those great eyes resting momentarily upon her. Angel and Thad were caught up and held in turn, too.

"Will you ride with me?" the old Basque asked Joseph, his voice betraying his uneasiness. He addressed the boy, but his question was really put to Grimm, and as he waited for Joseph to answer he did not take his eyes off the crow.

It appeared to Necia that Joseph hesitated as if expecting the somber bird to answer Angel. Suddenly she saw the crow spread his wings. A piercing, raging "Caw-w-w, Caw-w-w!" shattered the stillness, and with a sweeping rush Grimm sailed into the air.

Necia threw up her arm to shield her face as she saw him pause on high and drop like a plummet. But it was down on Angel that the cawing fury swooped.

The old Basque cowered in his rig, apparently unable to reach out for his whip. His team, however, had heard that rush of angry wings, and with a wild snort the horses lowered their heads and dashed away.

Necia saw Angel awaken from his trance and grasp the reins. A few seconds later, man and team were lost in the night.

Old Thad was searching the sky for a sight of Grimm. The crow's cries were rapidly growing faint in the distance. Thad listened, straining his ears until that wild cawing no longer reached him.

He looked for Joseph, but the boy and Slippy-foot had gone. He turned to Necia then, and they stood and stared at each other almost as if expecting to find that the strange trinity—Joseph, Slippy-foot and Grimm—had left some visible mark on them.

Without speaking they entered the house. Thad threw open the doors and windows. Necia followed him with her eyes, wonder growing in them as she saw her grandfather give way to his rising anger.

"I want air! *Air*—do you hear? Open up everythin'! Git the smell of them things out of here," he raged.

The plate that Grimm had touched with his bill in salvaging the bread crust caught Thad's eyes.

With an oath he picked it up and hurled it to the floor.

"Grandfather!" Necia protested.

"He ate out of it—that damned crow!" Thad shouted.

CHAPTER XIV.

THE BULLY.

THE memory of Necia stayed with Joseph and in the days that followed he pondered at length over what she had said. He was as far as ever from accepting her creed of life, but due to her a week passed before he thought of going to see old Angel.

He had begun to wonder what the business might be that had brought Thad Taylor and his grandfather together. This matter was soon explained to him in full by none other than Peter Organ, on his way north again. Peter was wrathful.

"All nice boys," he said, "the whole four of 'em. Been workin' hard, improvin' their land, and just about ready to ease up a little with the money from this year's wheat. Now they ain't got nuthin'. They'll have to sell—or starve. Five years' work thrown away. I could-a told 'em they was fools to go on workin' that-a-way, and nuthin' but a promise that they'd have no trouble about renewin' their leases. Humph!

"But I reckon if a hog ever got more'n he could eat, he'd spoil what was left. There ought to be a law ag'in 'em. And Thad Taylor joinin' in with Angel after all the yappin' he's done about the boscos! Makes me sick!" Peter snorted.

"Do not take it too much to heart, my friend," Joseph counsélled. "I assure you that neither my grandfather nor Thad Taylor will profit by what they have done. Martin Creek will be dry before August comes."

Peter just looked at Joseph pityingly.

"You—you don't really believe that, do you, Joseph?" he asked sharply.

"I do—beyond a doubt. It cannot be otherwise. Whatever your plans are, mold them accordingly. No rain fell last month; none will fall this month. And it is only the beginning. You should be able to recognize the signs."

"It *does* look as if we was in for a dry spell," Peter admitted; "but no man can remember when they wa'n't water in Martin Creek—not even Injuns. It's hard for me to believe that it's a-goin' to be as bad as you say."

"You are not alone in that," said the boy. "What did they say about me in Paradise when you told them I was Joseph Gault?"

Peter shook his head solemnly.

"I didn't tell no one that," he exclaimed. "I

got to figgerin' it'd be best for you to tell 'em when you was ready. It was gittin' hard for me to hold my tongue, so I lit out."

"I am glad you said nothing. Since I saw you last certain things have made me change my mind. But they will find me out soon enough. I may need you, Peter. Will I be able to find you?"

"Sure! I'm goin' over into the Pine Forest range. If you need me, send word to the Pingree ranch. They'll know about where I'm at."

And without further understanding they parted. Early the next morning, Joseph started for the ranger's cabin on Powder Creek. He needed salt for his sheep. Peter had told him that Heaton, the ranger, had salt for sale, and so, although Paradise was nearer, he set out for the Reserve.

Joseph had never been to Heaton's cabin until now, so he did not know that the Basque herders in the Reserve made it their rendezvous. Heaton made some small profit off them and, accordingly, suffered them to do about as they pleased.

Whatever supplies Angel sent to his men were left at the cabin. Hence, it became their headquarters, and on the morning that Joseph approached it Andres and at least a dozen others lounged about the place. Most of them were young—Felipe was one of them—and, as is the way with young men the world over when free of restraint, they were having a very merry time of it, indulging in pranks on one another, and proving to the best of their various abilities that herding sheep does not make Jack a dull boy.

An hour before Joseph reached the cabin, a Basque named Juan Icherraga, on his way to Paradise, had arrived with a small *remuda* of horses, among which was a wild-eyed piebald mare. She was a bucking horse that had changed owners many times. Icherraga had some local reputation as a *vaquero*, and it pleased him to awe his friends by showing them his mastery of the mare. He finished with a flourish, believing he had captured his audience, but Andres, who knew something of bucking horses and who had been watching him jealously, smiled scornfully.

"It is nothing," he said in Basque. "There is no fight left in the horse."

Icherraga put a hackamore on the mare's nose and dared Andres to ride. This was exactly what the big man desired. Vaulting into the saddle easily, he sent the animal away with a wild whoop. She bucked almost immediately, but Andres fanned the air with his hat and dared her to do her worst. In ten minutes he brought her to a halt in front of Felipe and the others.

He had not been thrown. They cheered him, and in other circumstances Andres would have been glad enough to have appeared a hero in their eyes, but now he saw more pleasure in heaping ridicule on the unfortunate Icherraga. The crowd was soon with him in this and, to complete the man's humiliation, Andres insisted that the boy Felipe could ride the mare. Felipe, however, was afraid of the horse and when Andres urged him to ride he shook his head determinedly. The crowd tittered now at Andres's expense.

"But I said you would ride the mare, and you will," he shouted.

"I—I am afraid, Andres," Felipe protested. "I know nothing of horses. I will be thrown."

"No!" the big fellow cried angrily as Felipe tried to dart away from him. He caught the boy by the neck and gave him a blow that sprawled him in the dust.

"Get up!" Andres commanded, and he half pulled the boy to his feet. The young Basques glared at the bully, but they were afraid to go to Felipe's rescue. Only Icherraga protested. Andres pushed him aside.

"Will you ride the horse now?" he bellowed.

Felipe cowered as he saw him raise his fist once more. But even so, the boy's fear of the horse transcended his fear of the man, and he cried out piteously:

"No!—no! Andres! I am afraid. Please—"

Andres did not wait for him to finish. White with rage, he grabbed the boy by the collar and dragged him toward the mare.

He was not aware of the newcomer who had turned the corner of the cabin and now stood regarding him with darkening brow.

*   *   *   *   *   *   *

It was Joseph. He had seen enough to understand what went on here. His arrival had passed unnoticed, so great had been the crowd's interest in Felipe and Andres.

"Let the boy go!" he cried.

At his call the bully stopped and turned angrily to find out who dared dispute his right to do as he pleased. The others were already staring open-mouthed at Joseph.

With widening eyes they saw Slippy-foot flashing around the flock until she had brought Joseph's sheep to a halt. Grimm had been perched upon the boy's shoulder, but he had tossed the crow to the ground, and as Joseph went up to Andres the great bird hopped along after him, cawing loudly and rolling his eyes menacingly.

To many of them Joseph had been an object of superstitious awe. One or two — despite the stories of Lope and his cousin—had believed him a ghostly visitant. Certain it is they feared him.

That this was due, in some measure, to tales of their own inventing, quite escaped them.

They had painted him in many colors, and with each telling their fanciful tales had grown, endowing him with strange powers and even producing those who had seen or heard him in communication with the spirit-world. Slippy-foot and Grimm had not been neglected in these idle vaporings, and they were commonly credited with being in league with the devil.

In fairness to Andres it must be said that he scoffed at these tales, for he was by nature a scoffer. Still, for all his skepticism, he was not past believing them.

The descriptions of Joseph had varied greatly, but now, although none of them had ever faced him before, it did not occur to a single one to question but what this was he who walked among them, finding him even stranger than they had pictured him. Icherraga was comical in his dismay, the whites of his eyes showing as he rolled them at Slippy-foot. As Grimm neared him, he backed away shielding his face with his arm. He mumbled something, but the crowd appeared not to hear him.

Joseph had surprised them completely, and if he had desired to awe them he could not have chosen a more dramatic moment for his appearance. But he saw only Andres and the helpless Felipe, and anger flashed in his eyes as he covered the distance between himself and the struggling boy.

Andres had stopped when Joseph called, and his face had blanched, but in the few seconds that passed before the boy came up to him he managed to recover his almost habitual sullenness. He waited until Joseph opened his mouth to speak, and then with a sneering laugh turned his back on him and started away dragging Felipe behind him.

The next moment he felt Joseph's hand upon his arm. He had not expected such strength and, caught off his balance as he had been, he could not help being whirled about.

"Let him go," Joseph said tensely. "He is afraid of the horse."

Andres's eyes narrowed beneath his shaggy brows. A snarl and a curse in Basque broke from his lips, and he sunk his fingers deeper into Felipe's neck.

"I'll not ask you again," Joseph warned as Felipe screamed. "I am unarmed. I have only my hands and my spirit with which to defeat you, but I ask for nothing more."

Andres's answer was only to curl his lips and bare his yellow fangs as a beast might have done.

Joseph did not wait longer. The crowd saw his right hand drop to his knee. With a swiftness that taxed the eye to follow, it came up, the weight of his body in back of it, and the next instant they saw Andres rock.

The blow had caught him on his beefy neck, and his head snapped back as if worked by a string. He hurled Felipe away from him as he struggled to keep from falling.

The blow would have been a knock-out had it been measured more carefully. Even so, Andres's eyes were blurred. He shook his head to clear it. A moment later he bellowed his rage, and with his hands outspread as if they were claws, he rushed at Joseph, not to hit him, but to tear and smother him, to stamp him into the ground. His face was hideous, his eyes glittering like an angry ape's.

Joseph leaped out of his way, and as Andres dove past him, he struck him again. Blood spurted from the bully's ear as he set himself for another rush. He was at least twenty pounds heavier than Joseph, and it seemed he must crush him as he leaped at him.

He was prepared to see the boy jump aside once more, but Joseph stood his ground and as Andres came on, his arms flailing the air, Joseph braced himself and drove his fist into the big man's middle. Andres stopped in his tracks, a horrible "whoosh!" forced from him as the air rushed from his lungs.

Joseph leaped in to follow up his advantage, but Andres caught him and held on, trying to smother him with his weight. Strength began to flow back into the Basque's arms. Joseph felt them tightening about him and try as he would he could not get free. Andres's weight also was telling on him. He saw that the man was playing for just that advantage.

Joseph beat his adversary's face into a raw mass, but Andres did not let go. He was a beast and he fought as beasts fight—willing to suffer now; content to bide his time. When he had Joseph flat on the ground he would repay those blows in good measure with his hobnailed boots.

The crowd wanted to see Andres whipped. At some time, each one there had felt his heavy hand. They had not dared to strike back. Joseph came to them as a champion out of the wilderness. They had proved themselves willing to believe anything of him in the past, and that he could crush Andres was quite within the possibilities.

They had overcome their fear of the boy, and they thrilled to see him punish the man who had bullied them so long. But now the advantage was Andres's and the crowd held its breath.

A grin twisted the big fellow's torn mouth as he felt the boy's struggles weaken. His eyes blinked open, and Joseph caught the thought which crept into them and made them gleam hideously, two spots of fire in a face from which his hands had beaten all human resemblance. To be dragged down now, was to be fatal, to be stamped to death. Andres had become the insensate killer—all beast—back into the slimy pit from which the first man had emerged still walking upon all fours.

And so they waited—one mad and the other with senses alert. Andres was past calculating his chances of victory. He was satisfied that he had won, and he could only hang on, knowing he had not long to wait.

Joseph, however, was watching—he told himself he was not to die here. Some opening, some advantage must come to him.

He felt his second strength flowing back to him, but he made no effort to break the big man's grip. Rather did he seem to struggle less and less. He gasped for air, and Andres grunted eagerly. Another minute or two and it would be over. Abruptly, Joseph seemed to go limp. Andres leered at him and, seeing the boy's eyelids close, he straightened up and let him sink to the ground.

But now the unexpected happened, for Joseph caught himself, and snapped erect. Andres tried to close on him again, but before his great arms could circle the boy's neck, Joseph's fist flashed up.

Every ounce of him—body and spirit—was in that blow. Energy he had not known he possessed, leaped within him. He could not have aimed and timed the blow better.

The crowd heard his fist thud against Andres's jaw, but Joseph had aimed beyond that, and the force of his blow, as he carried it through, lifted the big man's head. Almost instantly his body stiffened, and as his head had lifted, so now his body lifted until even his feet left the ground. The crowd gasped.

Andres's eyes were glazing. He was falling. He appeared about to go over backward, but suddenly his legs went limp. He crumpled up as a balloon does when the air is let out of it, and sank to the ground unconscious, blood trickling from his mouth and ears.

Joseph stood over him, swaying crazily, his chest heaving.

Felipe and the others came and stared at Andres.

"Ees he dead, *señor?*" Felipe asked, his face pale.

"No," Joseph answered. "Get me a bucket of water."

Andres stirred uneasily as Icherraga drenched him. Minutes passed, however, before he attempted to sit up. Slowly, understanding crept back into his eyes, and with it craftiness. Clumsily he lifted his hand to Joseph.

"You win, *señor,*" he mumbled. "But some day mebbe eet be my turn. You shake hands?"

Joseph shook his head slowly.

"No," said he, "I will not take your hand now. You have not changed. You are still the bully. What name are you called?"

"Andres," the big man answered sulkily. Joseph could not repress a start.

"So you are Andres, eh?" he asked, his voice chilling. The crowd as well as the man on the ground caught the intimation of previous knowledge.

"I am not surprised," Joseph went on, his eyes holding Andres's. He paused, then:

"Timoteo was right."

Only Andres understood him now, for the others had heard little of Timoteo. Joseph saw a question form on the big man's lips.

"It is nothing," he said before Andres spoke. "Can you get up?"

Andres tried to rise and Joseph reached down

a hand to help him, but the man's body had been too severely punished, and as Joseph let go of him he sank back to the ground. The smell of blood had drawn Grimm and, as Andres fell back, the crow hopped upon the man's chest and stretched out his neck, his bill clacking a foot from Andres's eyes.

Andres screamed and tried to move away, but it was more than he could accomplish. Joseph called Grimm and the crow backed off, cawing angrily as he retreated. Joseph was convinced that Andres was helpless.

"We will have to carry him into the cabin," he said to the crowd. "He will not walk to-day."

"But, *señor*, he must," Felipe announced. "He ees here weeth sheep. He ees on the way to my grandfather's *caserio*. We are but a few for so many sheep. I can not go. Eet be night before I get back."

"Sheep going to the valley so soon?" Joseph asked.

"*Si, señor.* Three hundred to be slaughtered. They are very fat."

One or two spoke to Felipe in Basque, but Joseph made no effort to learn what they said.

"Where is his flock?" he asked at last.

"Across the creek," Felipe replied. "The dogs are there."

Joseph pondered for a moment.

"Call in your dogs," he said finally. "It is my fault that he can not go. I will take the sheep to your grandfather — if you will trust me with them."

Felipe conferred with the others before answering. They seemed none too willing that Joseph should take the flock even though he had won their confidence.

"But you will need the dogs, *señor*," Felipe urged. "Three hundred sheep are too many for one man without dogs."

"No," Joseph smiled, "the dogs would not help me. Call them in."

And while Felipe was busy with the dogs, Joseph and two others carried Andres into the cabin. On coming out, he started his own little flock toward Buckskin. He then called to Slippy-foot:

"Home! Go home!"

The coyote stared at him perplexedly for a moment, but when Joseph repeated his command, she started off after her charges. The young Basques who saw this held it no less than a miracle. But they were herders, and peculiarly fitted to appreciate it.

When Felipe returned with the dogs, Joseph called to Grimm, and with the crow perched upon his shoulder, he crossed the creek. He soon had the big flock moving.

The young Basques watched him until he was lost to sight, marveling that in all that time not a single ewe had broken from the flock; not once had he been forced to stop for stragglers to catch up with the band. Sheep had never behaved that way for them.

So, although they realized now that Joseph was a flesh and blood creature, they found him an even greater mystery than ever. Sheep they could understand, but they could not understand him.

There is an old Spanish proverb to the effect that shepherds are foreordained to control the sheep. Felipe quoted it:

"*Dios los cria y ellos se juntan* (God brings them up and they get together)."

Icherraga exclaimed, "It is so."

CHAPTER XV.

"WE ARE FRIENDS."

JOSEPH drove the flock into the valley over the
road which dropped down from Hinkey summit.
In entering the Reserve this road ascended so
rapidly that it was little used, but for one returning to the valley this mattered not at all. It was
several hours shorter than the way that led
around by Antelope Springs, so when Joseph
arrived at old Angel's *caserio* it was still daylight.

The buildings which formed the *caserio* were
some distance apart. In them resided the families
of Angel's sons and grandsons. Set off by itself,
stood the old Basque's own house, surrounded by
barns, sheep pens and countless sheds, roofed over
but open on all sides, which served to house his
reapers and other machinery. Corrals were
everywhere—some of wire, some of brush.

On that long past day when he had been there
before, Joseph had been too young to notice how
well-conditioned the *rancho* was. It struck him
forcibly now. Everything was in its place; the
buildings freshly white-washed, the fences prim

and the stock—milch cows, pigs, horses and chickens—fat and healthy.

The usual odds and ends of broken-down hay-rakes and mowers which clutter up most ranch-yards were missing. The barns were free from litter. Indeed, look about him as he would, he could find no sign of waste. The place breathed an air of happy abundance, of tireless husbandry and frugality.

Only Andres, of all Angel's children, remained unmarried, so the great man was quite alone in his big house. But he did not lack for those to wait on him. This night he sat at his table in dignity befitting the head of his clan.

He heard Joseph drive the flock up to his door; but it had been expected all afternoon. Therefore, he did not arise. Others had noticed the flock, too, but believing the herder to be Andres they had gone on with their suppers. Hence Joseph passed almost unnoticed.

It was warm and he found the door open when he reached it. Angel dropped his knife and fork as he recognized him.

Joseph had long counted on facing his grandfather in this very room. In fancy, he had often seen the old man squirm before him, but the unexpected meeting at the Circle-Z had robbed him of that long-dreamed-of pleasure. However,

Angel's surprise at seeing him here, now, was genuine, and Joseph saw him draw back as Grimm stepped into the room.

"May I ask why you come here?" Angel questioned. "And that thing?" he cried, his voice rising angrily.

"I have brought the sheep that you expected Andres to bring," answered Joseph. "They are outside the door."

"What has happened to Andres?" Angel demanded, pushing back his chair as he got to his feet.

"Andres is a bully," Joseph declared flatly. "I had to rebuke him." And he told his grandfather what had happened at the ranger's cabin that morning. "I felt that it was my duty to bring the herd," he concluded.

Angel offered no word of defense for his son as Joseph told his story, and now he walked around the table in silence, his eyes on the floor. If by any chance he compared the youth before him to his surly son, and cast up a balance in Joseph's favor, no sign of it came into his eyes.

The room had been Angel's sanctum so long that it seemed to have taken on something of his personality. Tables and chairs gave evidence of an uncompromising fight with dust, for they had been scrubbed and scoured so often and so thoroughly that paint had long since ceased to adorn them. In fact, the pleasant odor of freshly scrubbed wood pervaded the room.

The walls were bare, and undoubtedly helped to convey the feeling of severity which the eye felt. A row of old tankards hanging suspended from hooks above the sideboard gave the room its only note of color.

In the corner stood a spinning-wheel (still in use whenever Angel's daughters returned to the parental roof) and beside it a great bag of washed wool ready for the wheel. A gigantic fireplace, fit to cope with the severest winter, occupied a good share of one side of the room.

A seven-pronged candelabra of beaten silver stood upon the table at which Angel ate his meals, its home-made candles standing somewhat askew and reminding one of a badly trimmed clipper ship. In forty years this room had changed but little. There was nothing in it to suggest America —not even a talking-machine. Nothing was "new"—veneered. Joseph liked his grandfather better for that.

"Did Felipe and his cousins know you?" Angel asked as he paused abruptly.

"I had not spoken to them until to-day," Joseph answered.

"And yet they trust you with three hundred

sheep?" the old man muttered, shaking his head as if unable to understand from whence their confidence sprang.

"They have no reason to regret their faith in me," Joseph said pointedly. Angel chose to ignore this.

"How much do I owe you?" he asked.

"You owe me nothing. I went to the ranger's cabin to buy salt. I will ask you to sell me what I need."

Angel did not say no or yes to this. The sheep were calling nervously, and the old Basque went to the door and ran his eye over the flock.

"Where are the dogs?" he demanded.

"I had no dogs—nor any need of them," Joseph replied.

"You brought this flock from Heaton's cabin without a dog?" Angel asked incredulously. Joseph nodded, but his grandfather found it hard to believe.

"The day has been hot!" he exclaimed. "It is a long way from here to the ranger's cabin. My herders can not drive my flocks that distance in the heat of the day. I have herded sheep myself. I know you can not drive them all day long in the blistering sun."

"But I did not *drive* them," Joseph replied without raising his voice. "They followed me."

"What? Three hundred yearling ewes that have never seen you before—followed you?"

"Three hundred or three thousand—it matters not: they follow me. Your sheep are fat and soft. And yet, I bring them to you as fresh as if they had not moved off their range."

The tradition of sheep was in the Basque. He knew their habits, their wants. Times almost without number he had proved his knowledge of them. The worries of lambing-time, of shearing, of fighting the storms of winter to get his herds under cover, of the long summer with its blistering heat, of breeding, of feeding—he had known them all. But here was an unbearded boy telling him he had done what sheepmen knew could not be done.

"But the *pinguey*—the rubber-weed—it grows thick along that trail? Andres has often lost a dozen head because of it."

"These sheep have eaten no rubber-weed," Joseph declared slowly. "They would be suffering now if they had. But you can walk among them, and you will not find one bloated ewe."

"You know the *pinguey* then, eh?"

"I do," Joseph said simply. "My sheep have grazed where the little yellow flower blossomed all about them, but they did not touch it."

"But my sheep have died from eating it," Angel insisted.

"Your herders were to blame. God never turned an animal from His hand altogether helpless. Sheep have instincts. If they eat *pinguey* it is only because they have been kept on one range too long—they are starving."

Angel stared at him in amazement.

"You—are only a boy," he grumbled, "how do you know these things?"

"I am a shepherd," Joseph replied. "It is in my blood. My father's people were shepherds. My mother's people—" Joseph stopped abruptly and, fixing his eyes on Angel, he said naïvely:

"I would like to talk to you about my mother and the people from whom she sprang. I—"

"No, no," Angel cried, aghast at the turn the conversation had taken. "It—it would prove nothing," he muttered, his face whiter than usual. "I am a sheepman. It is enough. I know sheep. Until now I would have laughed had any one told me they could be driven so far in June. I—"

"You forget," Joseph interrupted. "I did not drive them; they followed me. But they are tired. Where shall I put them?"

"The brush corral," Angel answered, indicating the desired one with his hand. Joseph nodded and moved away, the big flock eddying about him.

"Wait!" Angel cried. "I will get my men. You can not put them in by yourself."

A patient smile flitted across Joseph's face.

"It is not necessary to call your men!" he said. "I will put the flock into the corral."

"Alone?"

"Alone," Joseph replied. "In spite of your boast, I see that you know very little about sheep."

Angel could afford to smile at this.

"You with twenty sheep say that to me with thirty thousand head? I have corralled more sheep in one day than you have in all your time. You can not put those ewes inside without help.

Joseph did not reply to this challenge but without further ado opened the gate and marched into the enclosure. Without a word from him, the sheep followed, fighting each other in their eagerness to get within the corral.

A great dust arose, but Joseph made no effort to leave. The old man heard him crooning some strange melody. One by one the sheep began to lie down. Within ten minutes the entire flock had bedded for the night.

It passed belief. More than a hundred times Angel had watched his sons struggle for the better part of an hour to corral a flock no larger than this. They had always had dogs to aid them.

But here was this boy, single-handed, not only putting the flock inside the corral, but gentling it for the night. And all that in less than ten minutes!

Angel was awed. He trembled as he saw Joseph close the gate. What manner of person was this?

"In all Spain there is not such a one as he," the old man gasped. "It is as he says—he *is* a shepherd. See! They lick his hand as he passes."

And now as Joseph walked away, one ewe stuck her head through the brush and bleated, and although Angel had heard thousands of sheep call, he had never heard before such a cry as reached his ears now. This long drawn "Ba-a-a-a!" was sad, plaintive, almost human in its pleading.

"They love him," Angel grumbled to himself. "Look at him! He walks as though he owned this *rancho*. And his eyes—" Angel shivered. "What *is* this power he has over men and beasts? Can it be that the hand of God is upon him? Has he come here to haunt me?"

He knew that he feared Joseph. With an effort he tried to shut from his mind the memories that came surging over him, but even as he steeled himself Grimm, the crow, brushed past him, laughing rather than cawing, and Angel shrank back.

He was glad to see one of his grandchildren, a lad of fifteen, come running now. Angel ordered him to get the salt for Joseph. Grimm had perched himself upon the boy's shoulder, and the Basque eyed the ominous crow fearfully, but he invited Joseph to enter.

"You—are welcome to stay here the night," Angel said when they were inside. "Shall I have a bed made ready for you?"

"No," Joseph answered.

"At least, you will eat at my table—you will break bread with me?" Angel urged. The Basque was holding true to a custom as old as his race—that whoever came under his roof should be asked to break bread and eat his salt. He hoped Joseph would refuse, for he was anxious to see the boy gone. He had determined within the last ten minutes that he must devise some means of getting him away from Paradise, and he wanted to be at it immediately.

Joseph understood the reasons that prompted the man's offer of hospitality, and he answered accordingly.

"I will let my friend decide that," said he, nodding to Grimm who had perched himself upon the mantel above the fireplace. "Come! What is your answer? Is this house for us to-night? Can we share this man's food?"

The crow blinked wisely at Joseph for a moment and then tapped his way across the mantel until he stood almost directly above Angel. The Basque heard him stop, and he flung his head back as if fearful that Grimm would light upon him. But the crow only peered into Angel's eyes, apparently probing them for the truth, and as his malignant, questioning orbs scrutinized the old Basque, Angel shook. Joseph could see that the man suffered.

Suddenly, Grimm lowered his head and a blood-curdling: "Caw-w-w, caw-w-w!" broke the evening stillness which had settled over the silent house. Angel's jaw sagged as if his muscles had lost their vitality.

With hands upraised, he backed away, and he did not stop until he brought up against the dining-room table. Grimm fluttered to the floor and with a series of angry caws marched out of the room with never a backward glance.

"The answer is plain," Joseph announced; "our place is not here. I will pay you for the salt, and go."

Angel drew the air back into his lungs and with his foot he closed the door lest the crow might return.

"Put the money on the table," he said to Joseph, his voice shaking. "And never let that crow come here again. It is a thing of the devil. Why is it always with you?"

"We are friends," Joseph answered.

"Friends?" Angel asked, the word drawn out. "A scavenger bird!" He put all of the contempt and bitterness he could command into his voice. Tempting fate, he rushed to add:

"And you—with your power over animals and fools—why have you come to Paradise?"

Joseph did not answer at once and even before he spoke Angel regretted his question, because what he saw in the boy's eyes told him that his worst fears were to be realized—that Joseph had come back to avenge his father and mother.

One wonders if Joseph sensed what went on in the old Basque's mind. When he spoke, his words confirmed the other's fear:

"I believe you know why I am here."

Angel heard him drop a piece of silver upon the table as he went out, but the old man did not look up until the sheep bleated as Joseph passed the corral. He went to the window and peered out at them. Two or three of the ewes had thrust their heads through the corral fence, and they called and called as Joseph disappeared in the dusk.

Angel threw up his hands impotently and, although he was not a profane man, a curse escaped him. The sheep kept up their bleating, and in a growing rage, he rang a bell for his men to come and stop them.

The following hour found him resolved to erase Joseph at any cost. He had thought himself done with the curse the Gaults had put on him, but here it was again. All he had suffered; the lengths to which he had gone—had it been for nothing?

CHAPTER XVI.

"I AM NOT AFRAID."

MIDNIGHT came, but Angel sat slouched down in his chair. His thoughts were chaotic. Wearily he cast about for some way to get rid of the boy, and out of the welter of his thoughts Necia Dorr appeared before him. She was young and lovely. He had seen her eyes melt at sight of Joseph. And the boy had not been blind to her charms. He had fallen back, humble before her.

Thus a plan matured in Angel's mind. Morning found him closeted with old Thad at the Circle-Z.

"He must go," Angel insisted. "It does not rain. My people tremble before him. He is in league with the devil—that crow, that coyote— they make my flesh crawl! You saw how your girl greeted him. He is a romantic figure to her. You are not going to risk having him win her from you, eh, *señor?*"

"Ain't no danger of that," Thad declared, somewhat injured.

"But they are of an age," Angel argued, ignoring Thad's indifference. "Do not forget that this boy has an education. He is no fool. In every way, he is her equal. She will turn to him—it is inevitable.

"Why—it took them the better part of an hour to wrap a rag around that lamb's leg the other night—what do you imagine kept them so long? It was like meeting like. I tell you education sets men and women apart. Those two feel a common bond between them already. Where did your granddaughter ride to yesterday?"

Angel was taking a chance on this, but it hit the mark.

"She went up the mountain," Thad had to admit.

Angel threw up his hands, inviting Thad to draw his own conclusion.

"But she don't know who he is," the old cattleman went on presently. "When I tell her that he is Joe Gault's boy, she'll cut him dead."

Angel shook his head, pitying Thad for his denseness.

"No," he muttered. "You will drive her into his arms if you tell her that. She'll look on him as a persecuted man. Don't bring up the past. We can get rid of the boy.

"If she is interested in him, she will be anxious to warn him that he must leave—that people are threatening him already, blaming him for the drought. My friend—you do not want to see her married to such a man. No! Nor will you stand idle while she rushes headlong into an affair that can only break her heart. We must act."

Horror at what Angel pictured grew on Thad.

"I thought I was through with everythin' of the name of Gault," he ground out dully. "To think that I had to wait for some one to tell me what I ought to have seen myself. God!" He snapped erect in his chair suddenly. "What am I goin' to tell her?" he demanded.

"That the Basques are making threats; that men are talking of nothing but him; that they blame him for the plague that has come upon us— that they will destroy him if he stays."

Thad got up and called Necia, but he shook his head as if doubting his ability to convince her. His excitement was immediately communicated to the girl, and she listened with growing apprehension to what her grandfather had to say.

When he had finished she sank into a chair and gazed from one to the other. Anger flashed in her eyes for a moment as she began to comprehend what they proposed. Disgust, and pity for their clumsy trickery, followed.

"So you fear him so much," she murmured. "No, no; grandfather, I am not fooled. This boy is in no danger. Both of you trembled before him the other evening. For some reason, he is in your way. I will not be a party to your scheming."

"You will obey me!" Thad thundered. "What is your interest in this man? You're not in love with him, be you?"

"*Love?*" Necia echoed, shaking her head at the word. "No—hardly love, grandfather. But when I listened to him, I knew that I heard—truth. Peace came to me. I—I wanted to lift up my head and sing."

Thad and Angel stared at her as she stood before them with eyes half closed, her lips parted. Her grandfather needed no urging now, reading into her naïve confession the very thing which Angel had warned him of.

"Think what you will," he roared, "you will ask him to go!"

"No—no, I will not, grandfather," Necia declared without wavering.

"You defy me?" Thad snapped. "In all things you have had your way, but this once you will do my biddin'!—or you will leave."

Horror transfixed Necia's face as she heard this ultimatum.

"Grandfather—you—you do not mean that."

"I do!" Thad cried. "Will you obey me?"

Minutes passed before Necia moved. Slowly then, she nodded her head. In a voice so low that the two men had to bend forward to catch it, she said:

"I will go."

Without another word she turned and left them. Thad and Angel sat without speaking for some time. Later, they heard Necia ride away. They stared doubtfully at each other.

"She is gone," Angel finally said in a low tone.

"Yes—she is gone," Thad answered dully.

Could he have seen the light which shone in Necia's eyes as she sent her horse up the mountain-side, he would have had good cause to regret his decision. The day before she had ridden this very trail, and now she let her horse have his head whenever the way opened before her.

A sublimity that comes to but few wreathed her face. In the last half hour, she had made the first great decision of her life.

Slippy-foot scented her before she reached the coulee, and in answer to the coyote's bark, Joseph arose and scanned the trail. He recognized her while she was still some distance away. The speed at which she rode filled him with a vague sense of fear, and he caught her hand as she brought her horse to a stop in front of him. Her excitement and the long ride had put color into her checks, and Joseph trembled as he gazed at her, so fair and so much a part of the pink and white morning. Necia's eyes betrayed her agitation.

"You are in trouble?" Joseph asked, his voice heavy with anxiety. "Tell me what has happened!"

"It is hard for me to put it into words," Necia answered. "But it must be told. I have come here to warn you. Angel Irosabal is at the Circle-Z. My grandfather and he have determined to get rid of you. To hear them, your life is not safe. The Basques have united to drive you away. The drought continues and they curse you for it. . . . That my grandfather could stoop to this—"

"They can not hurt me," Joseph assured her.

"But you do not understand!" Necia exclaimed as she swung down from her saddle. Leaning against her horse, she said:

"This story is a lie. The Basques have not organized against you, nor have the other ranchers. My grandfather and Angel Irosabal are the only ones who have joined hands to get rid of you. For some reason they fear you. This tale was manufactured for my benefit. They hoped to trade on my expressed liking for you to get me to come up here and plead with you to leave. I refused to come on those terms. My grandfather gave me my choice—either do as he said, or leave his roof."

Joseph's eyes glittered as he listened to Thad's threat against Necia.

"But you are here?" he queried.

"As your friend," Necia replied bravely, her eyes meeting his without wavering.

"My friend," Joseph echoed, "my friend. I hope you will never have cause to regret calling me friend. But Angel Irosabal and your grandfather—they do only what I had expected them to do. And this is but the beginning. Wait until another month has passed.

"It—it may be too late," Necia murmured. "Your life *is* in danger."

"I am not afraid," Joseph declared. "I fear no man. Need I tell you that I shall stay?"

"No, it is not necessary. I knew this would not affect you. I am glad it is so. I—would not have you go."

"But you must go back at once," Joseph urged. "I will not forget your kindness. Tell your grandfather that I thank him for his interest in my behalf, but that his sympathy is wasted. My place is here, and I shall remain."

"I—I am sorry," Necia murmured, looking

away that he might not see her emotion. "I can not carry that message."

Joseph saw her body become stiffly erect as she paused.

"I am not going back to the Circle-Z," she said then, her voice only a whisper.

Joseph was startled. As he grasped her meaning, he shook his head gravely. Necia raised her hand entreatingly as he hurriedly sought to urge her to change her mind.

"Please——" she murmured. "I have quite made up my mind to that. I am *not* going back. I will not be used as a pawn. That Basque, with his grinning death's-head, has bewitched my grandfather—I hate Angel Irosabal."

"So, you hate him, eh?" Joseph asked, a grim smile fleeting across his face. "Yet hardly a week ago, you chided me for no more—I wonder what you would say now, if you knew what Irosabal owes me."

Light came to Necia. No wonder the old Basque wanted Joseph run off!

"So, it is *he* who has wronged you!" she exclaimed. "I guessed as much the night you came with the lamb." Unconsciously her voice became grave as she went on. "Don't think that his threat is an empty one. He will gather the Basques about him to get rid of you. My grandfather will help him. If the drought continues others will join them. They will stop at nothing."

"I am not afraid," Joseph declared again.

"Oh, I know you are not. I think that is why I have faith in you. You, above all others, could bring happiness to this valley. But they will not have it—

"Well, you will not have to face them alone. My grandfather drove me here—and here I shall remain! I came to warn you and I shall stay to help you."

Grimm, the crow, stood nearby with the gravity of an ambassador. Then—his penetrating, black eyes fixed on Necia's face—he spread his wings, arose a little way—and slowly, gently, settled at her feet.

CHAPTER XVII.

"MY PLACE IS WITH YOU."

EVENING came on. All afternoon long Joseph had momentarily expected Necia's grandfather to appear and demand that she return with him.

Joseph wondered what went on in the valley, for the fact that old Thad delayed his coming, only augured that he was organizing his strength. Surely the man could no longer believe that Necia had spent these many hours in trying to convince him that he must leave Buckskin.

Or was it Thad's plan to stay away until morning, thereby forging a weapon out of Necia's being there over night with him that could be used with telling effect in the valley? Armed with the tale that he had kept the girl a prisoner, Necia's grandfather might well hope to arouse his neighbors so that they would not hesitate at anything.

Prisoner she might have been throughout the day without arousing any neighbor's wrath, but over night?—No! Just why the friendly night should make such a difference in men's eyes it is hard to say. It was true, nevertheless.

Necia caught Joseph's thought.

"I—I understand," she murmured. "Night is at hand. But—I am not afraid to be here with you."

The desire to have her stay was born on the instant in Joseph. He gazed at her long and earnestly before he said:

"No—you have nothing to fear. If you will stay—you will stay. But there is one thing that I have left unsaid that must be told now."

"It can make no difference to me," Necia declared.

"It may," Joseph paused. "I am Joseph Gault —the son of the man who is supposed to have killed your father."

"Joseph Gault!" Necia's whisper was unsteady. He saw her draw herself up, her eyes closing. "Joseph Gault!" she whispered his name again, conjuring what pictures she alone knew.

"You see," he said gently, "it—it does make a difference. As you have said to me—I understand. You are free to go."

"No, Joseph," Necia answered, and her eyes sought his beseechingly, "I was not thinking of going. I haven't forgotten what you told me that night you came to the ranch. I do not accuse your father. I—I was just thinking how strange it is that you and I should be here together."

Her voice trailed away with her thoughts. Joseph grew silent, too. He could appreciate what she inferred. Their being there together was strange, indeed. Tabor Kincaid would not have believed that such a day would come. Joseph wondered what his mother would say if she could look down and see the two of them there, the night closing about them.

"Together . . . and friends," Joseph murmured half aloud. Necia gazed at him tenderly.

"And friends," she barely whispered. Her voice seemed to break, and Joseph looked up quickly—puzzled.

"We—*are* friends, Necia," he said rather sharply, alarmed at what he believed was a note of indecision in her voice. Necia looked away, and Joseph caught her hand impulsively and gripped it as if hoping by the force of his fingers to make her face him again. He felt her tremble.

"I—I am *your* friend, Joseph," she whispered, but she held her head turned away.

The vagrant night wind sent a strand of her hair against his lips. Joseph winced, but he did not release her hand. A mad desire to sweep her up into his arms and crush her to him almost overcame him as he gazed at her, so fair and so lovely.

"You—you are hurting me, Joseph," Necia murmured.

Hurting her? Could love hurt? Was this wild singing in his veins, this tumultuous pounding of his heart—was this love? A moment ago he had stood before her calm, poised, the master of himself; but that fleeting moment had been swept back into a dim past—lost—forgotten!

Had he been blind—dumb—that he had not felt the witchery of her beauty, the magnificence of her spiritual self, eating into his consciousness like fire? When he had fallen back before her, that night at the Circle-Z, had he asked himself why?

His spirit had bowed to hers then. He knew as much now. He had found her beautiful, her eyes lighted with a radiance truly sublime. This day had only further revealed the true nobility of her.

And she had come to him! Out of the welter of his thoughts he grasped that sustaining fact— she had come to him! What mattered it that it was night; that Thad Taylor and old Angel were doubtless rousing the valley against him?

Down through the ages, from the time when his ancestors had clothed themselves with the skins of savage beasts, the strain that was in him had been unafraid. They had taken their mates and held them—fought for them, fended off evil, died for them when circumstance demanded.

He knew that he was not the first of his strain who had stood at bay on the mountain-top, with the woman of his choosing at his side, defying the world. His own father had done no less.

He bent over and gazed into Necia's eyes. Mists swam in them. A cry escaped his lips. He released her hand only to reach out and draw her close to him.

"Look at me, Necia," he pleaded. "Tell me—are you afraid?"

Necia lifted her head, her eyes closed, her lips moving tremulously.

"No—I am not afraid with you, my Joseph," she said softly, her head shaking ever so slightly.

"You know that your place is here?"

Again she nodded.

"I—know," she whispered.

Transformed, exalted, he held her. The seconds passed, but neither moved. In one mighty rush of wings Joseph had been lifted to a seat with the gods.

He felt himself unworthy and he could but wonder what he had done to deserve such implicit faith as Necia had in him. He searched his soul for an answer, and whatever of dross there was in him was burnt up, fluxed, lost, through love of her.

Necia's head was thrown back and her lips were

close to his; a divine temptation. From the very depths of his being the urge to press his lips against hers, to drink in their loveliness—a holy communion of her soul and his—welled up in him. He trembled in his ecstasy.

He drew her closer still—so close that her breath fanned his lips. If he held back now, it was not because he hoped to whip his thirst for her to a still whiter heat. This moment could never come again. It was to be saved, treasured. From it life must date. And now to stab him came a fear for her.

It was not of the past or of the present, but of the future—of the Unknown. Like lightning there flashed across his mind the memory of what his mother had sacrificed for love. He had seen her lonely, unhappy, cut off from her people. She had loved his father none the less, but she had suffered and died for love of him.

Could he ask this girl to do as much? She had left the roof that sheltered her, had turned her back on her own, to come to him, to share his poverty, to stand with him against his enemies. All that a girl of her years might be expected to hold dear she was willing to sacrifice for him.

Could he ask it of her?—dared he accept it? And yet here she was in his arms and ready to seal the bargain with her lips! A groan of utter misery broke from him.

"Necia! Necia!" he exclaimed. "Open your eyes. Tell me—why are you here—why have you done this?"

"Oh, Joseph, do not put me away from you!" she cried. "Would you drag the truth from me. You—you know why I am here!"

"I do, I do! But you see me in rags, in poverty; your grandfather is against me. What have I to offer you?—what but the misery my father offered my mother?"

"No, no, Joseph. I am not afraid of that," Necia answered, her voice full and clear in the deepening twilight. "My faith in you lifts me beyond the need of material things. I have no need of wealth, so long as I have you. There can be no unhappiness where love is—no unhappiness that can last.

"I make no sacrifice. My place is with you. Where you lead—I follow. There is no life for me without you.

"I have longed—waited for your coming. My heart recognized you before you had spoken. My grandfather knew it—Angel Irosabal guessed as much. Only you have been blind, my Joseph."

"Necia—" The pent-up longing of his heart

and soul cried out as he held her off, marveling at her innocence, her honesty.

"Does it matter that our fathers were enemies? —or our grandfathers? They had no just quarrel. Nothing has mattered here but money and greed and hate. No one has cared for this land. You—are going to change all that, my loved one."

"I?"

"Yes—you, Joseph."

He could only look at her, amazed at the heights to which love of him had carried her.

"From the first," he heard her whisper, "I knew you had come for a great purpose—"

"My mother—" he started to say.

"No, Joseph. Your purpose is greater—far greater than that. You are here to show all men the way to something better than what they have known. Maybe it is my task to show you how, Joseph."

How sweetly she said that! How patient! Her lips were parted—poised as if lingering upon his name. A whippoorwill flashed by them. Its plaintive call floated back. From afar came the lowing of cattle.

He drew her close. Something of the infinite transfigured her face. He felt her arms stealing about his neck. Life was brief—fleeting; happiness a will-o'-the-wisp.

To attain it—to live—he must achieve her. The friendly stars bent down. In tones far too faint to be called a whisper, he heard her say:

"Joseph—kiss me. I am yours. Tell me—tell me, my love, that you—"

His lips stopped her words. Again and again he kissed her. Exalted—on high with her he left the little world of men.

Grimm, the crow, circled about them unseen, unnoticed. The rustling of the young cedars in the rising wind went unheard.

Soft as the night was the velvet of her cheeks. She stirred in his arms, her breast rising and falling. He poured love words into her ear—strange phrases of his own making.

Necia smiled up at him. Life was good!

CHAPTER XVIII.

TWIN FIRES.

TIME often proves itself incapable of gauging life. It was so with Joseph and Necia. Neither knew how long they had stood there enthralled.

Slippy-foot, baying the moon, had called them back. Food must be cooked, the fires built up—matters little in keeping with romance, but vital, nevertheless.

It became Necia's task to contrive supper from such meager supplies as the dug-out held. She was supremely happy as she hurried about, Slippy-foot at her heels. She could see Joseph gathering dry sage. By the time she called him he had ready two great piles of it—one to warm the dug-out and the other for the watch fire at the edge of the coulee.

Necia did not realize the purpose of the two piles of brush at first—one hers, the other his—and Joseph guessed as much.

"They tell their own story," he said, "two fires where there has been but one. Your grandfather will be scanning Buckskin. He will see our fires.

He may come soon.   When we have eaten you can fasten the dug-out door.   I will sleep on the coulee."

Necia smiled at him tenderly.

"My Joseph," she murmured, "there is no need of a locked door."

Joseph put his arm around her and caressed her.

"No," he said slowly, "there is no need of one. If your grandfather comes——"

"If he comes he will take me away only by force," she exclaimed.

Joseph shook his head.   "No, Necia, he will not take you away from me.   You may change your mind—it may be advisable under certain circumstances—you may want to go.   That is always your privilege.   But grandfather or not, he will not *take* you.   I swear it."

Necia did not ask from whence his surety sprang, neither did she question it.   She knew that when he spoke, truth flowed from his lips.

The fare she had set out for him was coarse, but she had invested it with a rare flavor.   If the spoons were of tin, the cups cracked, neither cared nor noticed.   What mattered it so long as they were together?

The spell of youth was on both of them, and the firelight danced in their eyes as they smiled and laughed. Joseph told her about his boyhood there on Buckskin, of his mother and of Tabor Kincaid. Last of all, he spoke of his father.

"I have been very near him many times," he said, "but he does not know me. He was in Mexico when Kincaid spread his story of my death. The news did not reach him for months. He had no reason to doubt it. It made him only more determined to come back and crush my grandfather. And he will accomplish no less, and soon, too.

"My father struggled for years before fortune smiled on him. He might have been a rich man to-day had he chosen, but he has squandered his money for the favors it would buy. Every move he has made has been to one end. Angel Irosabal and every other Basque in the valley will be forced out of Paradise before winter comes."

Necia put down her cup slowly. His tone left no room for her to doubt that he meant what he said.

"Joseph!" she exclaimed, her eyes suddenly serious, "are you going to permit this to happen? An entire people must not be made to suffer for the wrongdoing of one man."

"And yet it is almost certain that they will. I —I know, Necia, that my father has been guaranteed that early this fall the State Forester will issue an order closing the Reserve to sheep. Long before then the drought will have burned up the ranges. When the order comes no one will question the wisdom of it. It would have been issued notwithstanding. The drought helps my father's plans, but it has had no place in them. It can end only one way, Necia. The sheepmen will have to go."

"But there will be no place for them to go. Stockmen will be needing every bit of range they possess—cattlemen I mean—in another month."

"Nothing could be truer. They will find themselves helpless. They will try Idaho—the Malheur Lake country—but it will avail them nothing. My father has options on many square miles of range there. They will have to go to him—or sell their flocks."

Joseph's tone betrayed his satisfaction with the prospect. Necia sat back dismayed, shaken.

"You—you know this and do nothing to prevent it?" she demanded, getting to her feet. "Do you think it just?"

Joseph caught her excitement and he arose and faced her.

"In many ways it is," he said. "The Basques have done my grandfather's bidding. They have followed him without question. You know my score against him is heavy. If I had nothing but the memory of what he did to my mother to turn me against him, I could not forgive him. She suffered because of him. My father suffered, and I have, too.

"And yet when I learned what my father planned I came back here—came as you see me now, ragged, poor, the friend of whoever would accept me, ready to do all that lay in my power to help others, asking nothing, willing to put aside my own ends. And why—? Because I hoped to find that my grandfather had repented, that he might show me by some sign that he had relented and made his peace with his God.

"I did not come asking amends. I wanted only to see that he knew his mistake. I was prepared to go to my father and dissuade him—"

Joseph shook his head as he paused.

"I—I expected too much," he went on, his voice grown sad. "I left this mountain a boy; I came back to it a man. Oh, I was eager to be back, Necia. I wonder if you can realize the feeling that gripped me as I crossed this very spot. Things that only a boy remembers came back to haunt me.

"A dozen times that day as I climbed the mountain I closed my eyes to picture my old home. Why I should have expected to find it still standing, I know not. A boy needs little reason for such a hope."

Joseph's voice trembled as he looked away.

"It seemed that I had left it but yesterday," he murmured. "I saw it so clearly—the bench outside the door where I had sat with my father, listening to tales fashioned for my ears alone; the old red Bayeta blanket—red as fire—that had covered me; my mother's chair before the fire place—how often I had been rocked to sleep in that chair—

"I dropped my pack and ran. It was evening. Nothing was changed. Even the old smells were recognizable. But the cabin was gone—not a sign left to mark the place where it had stood. I searched the draw bewildered.

"I even wondered if I had come to the wrong place. If the cabin had fallen to ruins some sign must remain of it. But there was nothing left— not even a stick or stone.

"It had been torn down—expunged—so that no man could say where my father and mother had lived. Later, I found this old door which hangs on the dug-out. It had been hidden away in the *malpais*. I should have known then that I had received my answer.

"Tabor Kincaid had placed a monument over my mother's grave. Together, he and I had built a picket fence around it. They were gone—erased as the cabin had been. My grandfather had left nothing to remind men that Joseph and Margarida Gault had ever lived.

"The desire to kill him welled up in me. I raised my hands to God asking for some sign that would stay me, and out of the shadows Slippy-foot came. She had not forgotten—old Slippy-foot!"

Necia slipped her hand into his as he stood looking down at the coyote.

"No wonder they love you," she murmured, nestling her head against him. His arm tightened about her and they stood without speaking for a minute. Necia broke the spell that held them.

"Joseph—do not think that I fail to appreciate what you have suffered, or that I am suggesting that your grandfather should not pay for what he has done. My thought is far from that. He *must* pay, but the only coin in which he can do so, that will be of any value to you, will not be forced from him by what your father proposes.

"I grew up in a home where the Basque was always reviled. And yet I have found them quite like other men. They have their leaders just as we do. Your grandfather failed them. Prove that, Joseph. It will be enough."

He caught her hands and wheeled her about so that she faced him.

"No, Necia!" he exclaimed, "it will not be enough! What you suggest *will* be proved. The message my mother left me made that certain. My grandfather has known from the first that my father was guilty of no wrong. But to shield his own son he accused my father."

"His son?—one of his sons killed—"

"One of his sons; yes. Even now the man is plotting against you as well as me. Do not ask me to be satisfied with humbling him. That day has passed. He can not be excused. He knew the truth and withheld it; condemned my father, broke my mother's heart. . . . He will not harm you, Necia.

"I hold his *honorable* name in my hand. At will, I can cast it into the mire. And the things he has slaved for—his riches, his crops and his sheep! You know what faces him there. He will have no hay. His wheat is burning up in the fields. His sheep will become a millstone about his neck.

"And best of all the day comes when his people will see that it is because of him that they suffer. He knows who I am. He does not acknowledge me, but he knows. He trembles when he faces me. I alone can intercede for him, yet he hopes to drive me away. He is to be pitied."

"His *people* are to be pitied. They are the

ones to suffer. It must not be, Joseph—it must not be—even if it means forgiving your grandfather."

"But that is more than I can do. Do not ask it of me. I go on—to the end, Necia. My grandfather meets a just fate richly deserved. I will not raise my hand to stay it."

"And yet—you will!" Necia exclaimed, her head thrown back, a rare smile on her lips. Joseph gazed at her wonderingly, troubled by her confidence.

"It would be a God-like thing to do," she went on. "Jesus of Nazareth said: 'Forgive them for they know not what they do.' You, my Joseph, will say no less. The day will come when the people of Paradise will know how you have been wronged. They will know that you forgave them when you held them in your power. Your reward will be great."

She closed her eyes as Joseph stared at her. "I see you leading them," she murmured. "They recognize you."

"Oh, stop! Necia! Stop!" Joseph cried, trembling as he fell back before her. "How can you say that to me, knowing what is in my heart? You are more precious than life to me, but I serve you best only as long as I am true to myself. If I could forgive him as you do; if I could rise with

you, if I possessed the nobility that governs you,
I might do as you ask. But my feet are of clay.
You inspire me, Necia, as nothing else has, but I
must go on."

"And yet you love me?"

"Madly. You are as my life to me. This must
not come between us. My way is your way even
as your way must be mine. In all things I would
follow you, but in this I can not. Do not draw
away from me, Necia. Let me take you in my
arms. God's hand is in this. The drought is of
His making. You must see that it is so."

"And God may give you further sign of His
will. The drought is bringing suffering to all.
Because of it, men who have been enemies must
become friends. To live, they will have to ask
help of each other. I—I do not despair, Joseph.
If you love me you will sacrifice your own ends.
Not for me, but for these others. It is not too
late. God will send you some sign if it is to be."

Joseph smiled faintly at her earnestness.

"You hope for the impossible, Necia," he said.
"Would you build a wall between us?"

"But if it should come?" she demanded. "If
God should send you some sign?"

Necia held out her hands beseechingly and Joseph, torn as he had never been, knew not how
to answer. Whole minutes passed without a

sound from him. The panorama of his life passed before his eyes. There could be no future without her. Come what may, he must not lose Necia Dorr. He knew she endowed him with qualities he did not possess. That any sign could come to him, he doubted. He was not an apostle. But if God should send him some sign?—some miracle?

Necia watching him saw a shadow cross his face. She thought his eyes softened. His mouth lost its severity. His arms opened for her.

"If it comes," he said, the words dropping slowly from his lips. "If it does, I will accept it. I will not deny it."

With a cry of gladness she felt his arms embrace her. Her faith in him was more than sublime. She did not doubt that the Divine Providence would answer her prayer. In some way Joseph would receive God's message.

She was only dimly conscious of his repeated good-nights. She felt his lips brushing hers and then he was walking toward his fire. She stood and watched him as he strode away, Grimm strutting along behind him.

A peace she had never known came to her. Joseph was so erect, so unafraid—going out to guard her! A strange warmth suffused her as she entered the dug-out. She stopped and glanced back through the window at him sitting beside the fire, gazing into its embers.

Tears flooded her eyes as she turned away. Since childhood she had been dreaming her dreams alone. Her gentle nature had missed the companionship of a mother. The Circle-Z functioned in a strictly man-world, and she had had to mold herself accordingly.

Even so, she had been a softening influence on the lives of those hardy men who rode for her grandfather, but they would not have understood the tears.which dimmed her eyes as she got to her knees. Nor would they have understood her prayer, for it was such an outpouring of soul as could come from only a girl whose heart had been starved, shut in.

It was not for Necia to know that Joseph stirred uneasily beside his fire, the memory of her on him. He had no thought of sleep. Strangely, he started when even a jack-rabbit moved out in the sage, but if the night-sounds caused him alarm it was only because of Necia. The fact that he was there guarding her, watching over her as she slept, peering out into the darkness beyond the circle of his fire aroused in him quite the same feeling that possessed primordial man back in the dim beginning as he squatted before the cave in which his mate had sought shelter.

He willed himself to put behind him any doubt of the future. Each day must be sufficient unto itself. The promise he had given Necia he would abide by, come what would. Any lingering doubt of this was stripped from him as he sat there.

Grimm seemed to sense his thought and, ruffling his feathers, he drew his head in and clacked his tongue with the very effect of a short chuckle. Joseph glanced at him shrewdly.

"Grimm," he muttered, "I almost believe you read me. What have you to say?"

The crow moved his eyes slowly and with a look of great wisdom began to walk around the fire. He stopped all of a sudden and without warning let out a shrill: "Ca-w-w-w!"

Joseph snapped erect. Some one was coming! He could not question Grimm. He called a warning to Necia and backed away from the fire.

Only one reason could bring a man up the mountain to-night. His jaws clicked at the thought. No man must come between Necia and him! Whatever the cost, there was no altering that.

There, beneath the stars, he would fight his battle for her. Waiting, hands clenched, he assumed the rôle for which his God had created him—the defender of his mate!

CHAPTER XIX.

NIGHT FALLS.

WHEN noontime passed without any sign of Necia, Thad and Angel had begun to ask questions, and as the afternoon wore away the old Basque became more and more reluctant to face Thad's wrathful eyes. But the sight of him staring moodily across the desert at the mountain only infuriated the ranchman the more.

"I shouldn't never let her go," he snapped, and glared at Angel daring him to deny his words. Getting no answer, he marched out and rang the ranch bell, ordering his horse to be saddled.

"I ain't goin' to wait much longer," he growled when he came back to the house. "If she ain't here by dark, I'm a-goin' up there to get her."

The Basque scowled and got up and went outside muttering to himself. He was fully as much alarmed as Thad, but his agitation sprang from a fear that was no part of the old cattleman's anxiety. The question that obsessed Angel grew with the passing minutes, and when he heard Thad come to the door half an hour later, he turned to him excitedly.

"It is five o'clock," he exclaimed. "It is absurd to think it has taken her all this time to deliver our message. Do you suppose—that he has won her over?—that she has taken his side against us?"

"Are you mad, man?" Thad screamed. "I know that girl. She's nobody's fool. They ain't no turn-coats in my family."

"But he is no ordinary man," Angel replied, truculently. "I have begun to feel that it is possible for him to do anything."

"Talk—talk—talk!" Thad shouted.

"Yes—? Well, *señor*, I have seen him perform a miracle."

"What?—this dry spell?"

"No! Yesterday he led—led, not drove—three hundred sheep from the ranger's cabin on Powder Creek to my *rancho*. He had no dogs. It was hot. The *pinguey* grows thick along that trail, but not one of that flock ate it.

"Yes, and he corralled them, bedded them down, in ten minutes. No one helped him. Those ewes licked his hand. They called for him when he went away.

"And you—you have seen that coyote—a wild coyote, the breed we have always fought, the kind that has killed my sheep and pulled down your calves since we first came—you have seen him gentled, tamed, taught to herd flock.

"And that crow—that horrible crow—he has made him wiser than either of us. You know I speak the truth."

"That don't scare me," Thad declared emphatically, deceiving himself in his anger. "You got somethin' to fear him for; I ain't. He's just a man to me. It ain't my way to tell folks where to head in, but you have been ridin' herd on that boy, and on his maw before him, a long time. If you tremble now, that's *your* business.

"You came to me to help git rid of him. And we'll do it; but if you want me to string along with you, don't you put too much store in him tamin' animals.

"If you knew my girl as I do, you'd waste no time gabberin' about him turnin' her against me. I was pretty hard on her to-day, but she knows that's my way—that I got to do a little rantin' when folks try to cross me."

Angel was at no pains to conceal his contempt for his ally.

"Why does she not return then?" he inquired cuttingly.

"He's got her held a prisoner, that's why!" and Thad cursed violently. "He ain't a-goin' to move off without a fight. If you ain't blind, you must see what he's plannin' to do. He's a-goin' to hold her over my head—the damn gospel shark! I reckon I'll stop him short. He'll find he's dealin' with a man that won't be stopped by any side-show tricks. Soon as it gits dusk, I'm a-goin' to steal up there—and I'm a-goin' armed."

"But he will know you are coming. I will go with you—and we will go unarmed. We can not surprise him. The crow will warn him."

"Well, we'll go, crow or no crow, and we'll go armed! My good name is at stake. No man's ever had cause to question the wimmen of my family. God help him if he's put a hand on her. I ain't too old to use a gun."

"Yes, but guns are not popular to-day, my friend."

"If I was younger—if I was the man I used to be, there'd be no talk of guns. I'd go up there with my bare fists and git her."

"But you are old—and I am old—and this is a young man's job."

"There's no denyin' that," Thad admitted. Angel had no desire to face Joseph, and he hastened to take advantage of what he thought might be wavering on Thad's part.

"You—have your men," he prompted.

"Hell! My *men!*" Thad exclaimed contemptuously. "They think he's an apostle. What of your sons? Where's Andres?"

Angel hung his head.

"He whipped Andres yesterday morning. That is why he came with Andres's flock."

"That boy whipped Andres?" Thad demanded incredulously. "A man twice his size?"

"It is no use to deny it," Angel answered. "Andres could not walk."

"Well, it wa'n't a fair fight, I'll bet!" old Thad exclaimed. "It ain't possible. I've seen Andres fight. God, if he was only here now. I know him; I bet he's achin' to git even. He'd be the one to go up Buckskin. He'd git Necia—where's he at?"

The Basque shook his head at the implied thought.

"He is at the ranger's cabin or nearby," he said wearily.

"I can git him," Thad declared confidently. "My fencin' gang is camped out between Heaton's place and the stage-station on Powder Creek. They's a 'phone to the station. Duval will send word to my men. They'll git in touch with Andres. I'll tell 'em to let him have a horse. He can git here in two hours."

"It will soon be night," Angel demurred.

"All the more reason that we shouldn't stand here wastin' time. You ain't backin' down, be yuh? You was anxious enough to have me send

Necia up there. We're a-goin to go through with this play now."

"I have not changed my mind," Angel flashed back, his eyes snapping under Thad's lashing.

"Well, shall I git Andres?"

"Yes—if he will come. This thing might as well be settled to-night. Tell him I said he should come."

Thad left Angel staring up at Buckskin, a gray blur in the deepening twilight, while he went in to telephone. The instrument was one of the old-fashioned kind on which it was necessary for the party calling to ring for central, and Thad spun the little handle savagely. The din brought Little Billy, the cook, to the dining-room door.

"Sumthin' wrong?" he demanded, with the privilege of a trusted man-at-arms.

"If they ain't, they's a-goin' to be if you ain't out of here directly. What you standin' there gabbin' about?"

"Miss Necia—"

Thad slammed the receiver down.

"Say!" he roared. "Don't you be spillin' that to the boys. You'll have less hair than you got now and no job if you do. You git me?"

Little Billy grinned. He understood the symptoms. Something was decidedly amiss. He nodded his answer.

"Then git!" Thad shouted, turning back to the telephone.

He had no trouble in getting in touch with his men, but the forty minutes which passed before he heard the bell ring, announcing that the Powder Creek station was calling, reduced him to a state bordering on nervous exhaustion. The word which he received cheered him. Andres had left the ranger's cabin at noon on foot for the valley. He was going by way of Antelope Springs. That meant that he would be passing the Circle-Z ranch-house in the next hour.

Thad ran out to tell Angel, but as he approached the old Basque he stopped suddenly, for Angel was staring wide-eyed at two spots of fire twinkling far up the side of Buckskin. Thad felt the man's fingers tighten on his arm.

"See!" he pointed. "Two fires—his and hers. Your granddaughter is *not* a prisoner."

Thad's mouth popped open as he sensed the meaning of the twin fires. He swallowed deeply, a queer sound rumbling in his throat.

"It is an act of Providence," he mumbled, and Angel stared at him, at a loss to understand his meaning. "Andres left the ranger's cabin at noon," Thad went on then. "He'll be here within the hour. Told Heaton he was comin' to find him —Joseph! God!—he can't come too soon."

CHAPTER XX.

FATHER AND SON.

ANDRES came in due time, and he was surprised to find his father awaiting him. The son's face was still swollen and discolored from the beating he had received.

Thad stared at him, reading in his appearance the true story of the man's encounter with Joseph. The old cowman was still loath to admit the truth, but in the face of such evidence he could not deny it, and he pursed his lips nervously, his confidence in Andres's ability to rescue Necia undeniably shaken.

Angel spoke to his son in Basque, and Andres replied to him in the same tongue. Thad waited, thinking each was intent only on explaining his presence there, but as they ran on without any sign of consulting him, he exclaimed sharply:

"That's enough of that lingo. We'll talk English, so I can git a word in."

"I was asking him about his trouble with the boy," Angel said in an effort to appease Thad. "He says he was whipped fairly."

"How'd he do it?" Thad demanded. "You weigh nigh two hundred, Andres."

"I lose my head," answered Andres. "But eet ees my fault. I was wrong. I should not make Felipe try to ride those horse. I bear no grudge, though."

Angel and Thad flashed a glance at each other.

"Why I thought you was out to git him," Thad exclaimed. "I called up the station an hour back. We was lookin' for you. Heard you'd told Heaton you was comin' back lookin' for Joseph."

Thad had not yet explained his present interest in him, and Andres, remembering the past, answered sullenly:

"Mebbe that ees so, *señor.*"

"You ain't any too certain about it, be yuh? You ain't afraid of him?"

Andres grinned in a way that made Thad draw back.

"No," he muttered, "I—understand heem."

"You understand him," Thad repeated. "What do you mean by that?"

"I mean—I know hee ees my friend," Andres replied slowly, his face hardly less unlovely, for all that his eyes softened. "I have come to ask heem to take my hand."

"What?" Thad and Angel uttered the ejaculation as one man. Bewildered, momentarily crushed by what they had just heard, they dropped into their chairs, speech denied them. Could it be that this was their champion, the man for whom they had waited, the one who was to do their work this night—who was to drive Joseph away and restore Necia to her grandfather?

Andres glanced from one to the other, not understanding their baffled look. Anger began to surge in Thad and his face purpled, but Angel's was the color of chalk.

"Eet ees a surprise, eh?" the big man queried, not overly pleased with them.

"You—you're the man I sent for," Thad managed to utter at last. "Bah!" and he accompanied the exclamation with a frightful curse. "My girl's up there!" he roared. "My girl—hoodwinked by him—fooled by his fancy talk. You was to git her for me. She wouldn't be there if your father hadn't come with his palaver. He talked me into sendin' her; anythin' to git rid of that boy."

Thad raised his fist and shook it at Angel. "Look at him now—shakin' as if he'd seen a ghost. And you—tellin' me you're a-goin' to ask Joseph to forgive you! Say! Where do I git off?" Thad banged the table with his fist, his voice rising with rage. "Are you just a-goin' to sit here?"

Angel shook his head weakly.

"It is as I told you," he murmured; "First your girl, and now my son. One by one that boy wins them. You mocked me, but I spoke the truth. He's in league with the devil. I can feel him fastening on to me."

Angel got up, his hands working nervously. "I was against you this afternoon when you talked of going up there armed. Well, I won't stop at anything now. He's got to go. You let me talk to Andres. I'll call you when I'm done."

"Well, you'd better talk some sense into him," Thad retorted. He got up and started to leave the room, but he came back and opened his safe. Andres had dropped into a chair beside the table. Thad went up to him, a stack of twenty dollar gold pieces in his hand.

"I don't know how many's there," he exclaimed. "I've got more if I need 'em. I drove Necia away from this house. I want her back before midnight—and no talk." He spread the gold pieces in front of Andres. "Take 'em," he muttered, "but you git Necia for me."

The big fellow's eyes narrowed as he stared at the gold, but he made no effort to scoop them up, and as Thad left the room, Andres lifted the red cloth which covered the table and dropped it over the money as if desirous of removing the temptation. His father drew up a chair and studied him.

"My son," he began in Basque, "we are back to-night where we were twenty years ago. You have said you came to find this boy, to ask him to forgive you."

"That is true," Andres answered, slouching further down in his chair.

"No—no, Andres. It can not be. Do you know that he is the boy Kincaid said had died— that he is Joseph Gault?"

"Joseph Gault?" Andres barely whispered the name. Instantly his mind flashed back to what the boy had said to him. A haggard look crept into his eyes. His father saw his mouth twitch.

"There is no need of your answering," said he. "You must know what he has come back to do."

"Dorr?" Andres breathed.

"It is his chief reason. Dorr's daughter is up there with him. He won her over. This man, Taylor, is blind. The girl is in love with that man. I saw it when they met here a week ago. The boy hopes to hurt me, too. I feel it wherever I turn, but I tremble more for you, Andres. Did he say nothing to you?"

"Yes," Andres nodded. "He asked me what I was called, and when I told him he said: 'So you are Andres, eh? I might have known. Timoteo was right.'"

"Aw-w-w!" Angel gasped and shuddered. "He knows!" he said hopelessly.

"He can not know!" Andres replied with strange emphasis.

"That his father had nothing to do with Dorr's death?—he *must* know! And Timoteo—what does he know of him? What is this thing that Timoteo has said? He would not remember him —can it be that he has found the boy's body?"

Andres's head sagged down on his chest at the thought, and with each passing second he found it harder to refute it. Andres had never talked about Timoteo, and yet Joseph had hurled his brother's name at him with studied purpose.

Angel read his son's train of thought, and he echoed it. In his soul he knew his surmise was correct. No further explanation was possible, and the truth crushed him. He shook his head as Andres muttered unconvincingly:

"It can not be. We looked for Timoteo."

"It can be," his father replied. "The boy is not like other men. I can not deny it any longer —he has a power."

He told Andres how Joseph had brought the flock. This was something Andres could understand, but he only narrowed his eyes the more.

"You do not seem to understand, Andres," his

father went on. "If that boy has found Timoteo, if he accuses you—I am ruined. The drought continues. Soon I must borrow money. I've got to buy hay-land. I may even need to ask men for range. My name must not be blackened by what happened so long ago. And you, Andres—what must happen to you, if he talks—if he knows the truth?"

Andres held his breath until the air rushed from his lungs explosively, but the snarl that his father half expected did not follow. Andres's voice dropped almost to a whisper as he said:

"Maybe—I go to jail. Maybe I will be—be—"

"Yes, that. That is what it will mean, my son." Despair gripped Angel. "Back—back where we were twenty years ago. And I thought myself done with the Gaults."

Andres saw his father age as he sat before him. Pockets gathered beneath Angel's eyes; the hollows in his cheeks became deeper. Andres began to believe that he might die without ever leaving his chair. He was totally unprepared to see his father spring erect, something of his old fire leaping back into his eyes as his masterful will summoned the flesh.

"We will stop this to-night!" he exclaimed. "You are going up the mountain. Get this man's girl for him, but be done with this Joseph first. Taylor can not break with me. Between us, he and I have more to say about what goes on in this country than all the others put together.

"When we say that Gault's boy stole Necia Dorr men will remember how his father ran away after the crime. They will see his son come back to revenge himself on Dorr's daughter.

"You go! You will have guns. Use them if he will not give up the girl. When he raises his hand to stop you—end it right there."

Andres's eyes burned into his father's.

"So you, my father, ask me to kill him," he muttered finally, his tone chilling.

Angel clenched his teeth and pushed out his lips in an angry grimace. The words came with a whistling sound as he said:

"Between the two of you, I have to choose. He must die. You do not refuse to go?"

"No! No, I will go," Andres answered as he got to his feet, "but I must say what I should have said years ago. Behind my back my own people, even my brothers, have called me a coward —a bully—they have been right. I was just that. Timoteo knew. You have never heard the truth about what happened that night. I killed Dorr—"

"You need not shout it out," Angel protested.

"No one here understands—if they do, I care not—I shot Dorr. I did not go out that night to kill him. You know that is so.

"You had talked your hatred of the Gaults into me from the cradle. When Timoteo and I went up to run Gault's sheep across this man Taylor's line, we thought we were pleasing you. You were to blame. You do not have to shake your head, my father. I speak the truth for once.

"Timoteo was ahead of me. Dorr shot him. So I shot Dorr. I have often forgotten that, but I never forget that I ran away when my little Timoteo called to me. I left him there to die. A million times I have heard him cry: 'Andres, you are a coward!' I have heard it on the range when I have been alone. It is with me all the time— 'Andres you are a coward!' I saw him; I heard him—but I ran.

"I was a coward. I have always been a coward. I said nothing when you drove Margarida away. I let you put the law after this boy's father. Always I have been afraid."

"Stop—stop!" Angel groaned.

"We have much to be ashamed of," Andres declared. "But I am going to prove to you to-night that I am no longer a coward. I will go— as you ask. You have always told me of the honor of the Irosabals. Well, I will do my part for the Irosabals to-night. Call this man, Taylor. I do not want his gold. Call him!"

"Have you talked some sense into him?" Thad inquired as he opened the door.

"I will go," Andres answered for his father.

"Well that's—"

"And I will take your guns," Andres went on without heeding Thad's interruption.

"You have got sense, ain't yuh?" exclaimed Thad. "You take my guns. Strap 'em on yuh. Put 'em around in back of you. You'll have to walk up to his fire with your hands in the air. He won't think you're armed.

"If he tries to stop you—go ahead. Your father and me'll be behind you. But don't you come back without Necia.

"Don't look for trouble—go up to him as if you was his friend. You understand?"

"*Si, señor,*" Andres drawled. "I understand!"

CHAPTER XXI.

REVELATION.

NECIA had come to the door of the dug-out. Slippy-foot was standing with her nose thrown up to the wind, but she made no sound. Joseph had marked as much, and he was not surprised that Grimm, the crow, did not call again, for he had never found them divided in their opinions.

In four or five minutes Joseph caught the glow of the torch which Andres held above his head as he advanced. The light, held above him, kept the man's face in shadow and it was not until he was within fifty yards of Joseph's fire that the boy recognized him.

"Why are you here?" Joseph called. Andres had not yet made him out, for the boy had stepped back so far that the fire-light did not reach him.

Necia knew Andres by sight, and she stifled a cry on recognizing him.

Andres, in turn, recognized her, and to give him credit, he was not surprised to find her a free agent. The girl had the dug-out; Joseph's blanket was spread beside the watch fire.

"I—I come as a friend," Andres stated. He saw Joseph now and walked toward him. Grimm, the crow, had escorted Andres as he approached the fire. Joseph glanced at the bird before speaking.

"I have no reason to doubt you," he said then. "Grimm and the coyote do not protest your coming. What is your mission?"

"I come to offer you my hand again," Andres answered haltingly. "I—I was wrong yesterday."

The man's voice rang true, but the boy could not believe his ears. However, he cried, "Advance!" wondering if a miracle had come to pass. Was this man the coward—the bully—of yesterday? Andres came up to him, his great head thrown back. Joseph stood and gazed at him.

"You *have* changed," he exclaimed. "You are not the Andres you were yesterday."

Necia had come close enough to hear what Joseph said. He seemed engulfed by the significance of Andres's coming. Necia had said that God would send him some sign—some proof that he was to lead his fellowmen to a better understanding. Could he doubt that this was God's answer?

Necia was not slow to see what Joseph's thought was, and she thrilled as she saw the boy move forward to Andres.

"I offer you my hand, my friend," he said. "You are welcome."

Andres, however, seemed turned to stone.

"You call me friend?" he murmured. "Knowing what you know—you are willing to take my hand?"

"I offer it to you, Andres."

But the big fellow only shook his head.

"You are Margarida's boy—I know!" he cried. "And you have found me out. When you spoke about Timoteo, I understood. You have found heem, too. But that ees not what brought me here."

Andres dropped his torch as he finished speaking and his hands flashed to the guns which he had strapped on behind him. First his left hand and then his right came forward, each holding a big .45. Necia screamed a warning to Joseph.

"You have nothing to be afraid of," Andres said to her. "I was sent up here to get you. Theese gun belong to your grandfather. My father and heem ees wait at the Circle-Z for me. And Joseph—they theenk I come to keel you."

Andres flipped the guns around in his hands so that he held them by the barrels, and then without looking again at either Joseph or Necia he tossed the pistols into the sage.

"Andres!" cried Joseph. "You do that—believing I hold your life in my hands—knowing that I know who killed this girl's father?"

"Yes, Joseph, yes! I do anytheeng for you. You open my eyes!" A wild cry broke from the big man's lips and he flung himself to his knees before Joseph, pouring out his soul, denying no part of his guilt, of his meanness, finding peace at the feet of the boy he had been sent to kill.

"Eef you say, go, I go. I'm not afraid to die," he cried.

"Andres, you are clean. Arise!" Joseph commanded. "I forgive you. You need not fear that I shall be driven away. My father lives. He soon will make himself known. I will take you to him.

"The drought will continue. All of us must suffer, but we will lean on each other. You have opened my eyes, Andres. You, who were my enemy, and you, Necia, who might have been, are now my friends."

Joseph put his arm around Andres as he got up.

"And you?" Andres asked Necia, "you forgeeve too?"

Necia nodded, but she turned away, her eyes wet at the man's contrition.

"I told my father," Andres began again, "that I would try to prove to-night that I could do sometheeng for the good name of my people.

He misunderstand me. But I say to you, Joseph, I will keep my word. Soon I be the head of my clan. I am the oldest son. My father ees very old man. Eef he not change, I change.

"You are part Basque, Joseph. Me, I am all Basque. Theese girl ees no Basque at all. But eef we be friends, then all Basques can be friends."

"Andres, Andres!" cried Joseph, his heart smiting him with joy. "If I have helped you to see that, if I can help that day to come, I care not what else happens. Come with me!" and Joseph held out his hand and led the way to the dug-out.

And as the three moved away from the fire, Grimm, the crow, raised his wings and settled upon Andres's shoulder. Andres stopped and looked up fearfully, but Grimm's eyes were no longer ominous.

Joseph was in the dug-out only a second. When he came out he held the bottle containing his mother's and Timoteo's letters.

"Here," he said to Andres, "is the message my mother left to me, and here is Timoteo's. My mother buried him. She knew, and I knew, what you have told us to-night. Take them—destroy them!" and he handed the two letters to Andres.

The coarseness seemed to fade from Andres's face as his fingers closed over Joseph's. His eyes lost their piggishness; and as he watched the flames lick up the two pieces of paper he made the sign of the cross with his thumb.

"If you will stay here, my blanket is yours," Joseph said to him. "I will share it with you."

"I—I will stay," Andres answered.

And down in the valley, Thad and Angel waited. No one came. No sound of shooting broke the stillness. Night passed, and dawn found them hollow-eyed, old, silent.

First Necia and then Andres—Angel got down on his knees, daring to pray.

And Thad, the scoffer, turned away, his lips sealed.

CHAPTER XXII.

THE LEAN KINE.

MAN and boy, Thad Taylor had arisen with
the sun. Pagan that he was, he had drunk of the
dawn as though it were some healthful anodyne.
This morning, however, he shivered as he closed
the door on old Angel and stepped out to greet
the Host of Light.

The air was cold, as it ever is at dawn on the
mountain-desert, even in midsummer, but Thad
shivered not because of it. His was a mental
reaction. He did not know it as such, sensing
only that for the first time his spirit failed to
thrill at the wonder of the coming day.

He squinted his eyes, as was the habit with him,
and gazed far off to the east where the lofty Tuscaroras, swathed still in their night dress of filmy
blue, dissolving rapidly now into a silver gos-
samer, lifted their spires and turrets dripping with
deepest orange and cherry. Even as he gazed
at them the cherry warmed to rose, the orange
became yellow. Fire touched them suddenly.
They seemed to tremble with the wonder which

they withheld from the waiting world for a brief second.

Thad wet his lips. He knew the play by heart; the climax was to hand. Like a jack out of his box the great sun popped above the shimmering peaks. The blue and violet hosts scampered away. Valley and mesa floated in a golden sea, the hazy drapery of the night caught fire, flamed and was gone; and lo! it was day.

Out from the ragged *malpais,* a coyote leaped to the crest of the rimrocks above the cañon of the North Fork. Raising his head, he barked his obeisance to the God of Light. From afar his brothers and sisters answered him.

Thad heard a door open. The angry jangle of spur chains clanked metallically as the wranglers moved away to cut out the horses for the day's work. The smell of coffee came from Little Billy's fire; breakfast would not be long delayed. A window went up with a bang. Cursing followed—a broken shoe-lace!

On a thousand mornings had the Circle-Z ranch-house echoed to just such sounds. There was nothing in the day to mark it as different from those that had been, and yet Thad found it all wrong. He thought of yesterday. It seemed far away.

He wondered if he could ever get back to it——

back to where he had been before Angel had come with his talk. He damned him aloud, the while his eyes swept Buckskin.

MacNeil, the blacksmith, whistling a merry tune, came out and pulled the rope that turned the windmill into the wind. It began to creak and rattle.

"Stop it; stop that damn noise!" Thad shouted. Poor Mac looked at him askance, wondering if the "old man" were daft. The windmill had creaked and groaned daily for ten years without a protesting voice having been raised against it.

Thad saw the man's unasked question, and having no answer for it, he reëntered the house and left the hapless MacNeil to himself. The incident, trifling though it was, served to bring Thad out of the backwater in which he had been drifting since the evening before. At least he had been made angry with himself, and as he faced Angel his jaw held some of its old air of determination.

Angel did not look up as Thad entered. He sat slouched down in a chair, his head bent forward. Thad glanced at him twice, so still did the Basque sit. Thad could not see the man's eyes, but the whiteness of his knuckles as he gripped the arms of his chair told him that Angel was not asleep. This immobility exasperated Thad. He waited a minute for Angel to speak, but the Basque remained silent.

"You ain't a-goin' to sit there all day, be yuh?" Thad demanded in rising anger. "You had schemes enough when you came here yesterday mornin'. It's time to do somethin'!"

Angel nodded and said: "Yes."

"Well, pull up then!" Thad snapped, "Pull up! This damned inaction is killin' me. Sittin' here mopin' ain't a-goin' to git us nowheres. It's mornin'! I ain't wastin' no more time. You grab a bite, and we'll move."

Angel got up slowly, nodding his head as if confirming some decision of his own making.

"A cup of coffee will satisfy me," he said. "Have your men ready."

"You forgit my men!" Thad exclaimed impatiently. "Do you think they'd take my side against her? If she's up there because she wants to be, they'd see me in hell before they lift a finger. What do they care for their jobs? Where they'd git another one now, God only knows. But that wouldn't matter. They're a pack of sentimental fools. You and me started this thing, and we'll finish it."

Angel agreed wearily. In the full light of the morning his skin was yellow. His eyes burned with an unnatural brightness.

"Perhaps we had better make a friend of the boy," he said under his breath.

"Sure—anythin' to git rid of him!" Thad answered.

Joseph's grandfather curled his lips in a mirthless grin.

"I—I did not mean it that way," said Angel.

Thad threw up his head wondering if he heard aright.

"You mean—to lay down to him?"

"No; to compromise with him."

"Well, I'm damned!" Thad gasped. "You suggest that to me?" He shook with wrath.

Angel appeared not to mind. He took out his watch and wound it absentmindedly.

"I know what you do not know," he said slowly. "Andres had every reason for doing what we asked. But have we heard a shot? Has he come back? No; and he is not easily moved. What I said to you yesterday is as true now as it was then. This Joseph has bewitched the valley. He has made your granddaughter love him. He has turned my son against me, he has—"

"You're jest guessin' at that!" Thad exclaimed. "How do you know what's happened up there?"

Angel shook his head at him.

"I know," he muttered. "I feel it in here," and he tapped his breast. "Wherever that boy goes he makes his friends. I would not believe the stories I heard. I do now.

"For twenty years I have tried to forget the past. He is here to rake it up again. Well, if it is money he wants, he shall have it. I will stop at no price to get rid of him. Do you think I am going to see him turn my own children against me?"

"Well, that's what he's done to me, ain't it?" demanded Thad. "Do you think I'm a-goin' to stand for that? Give him your money; do anythin' you damn please, but I'm a-goin' to settle with him in my own way."

He ordered breakfast and horses, and with a curt gesture to Angel, said:

"We'll eat now."

Before they had finished, Race Eagan—one of the two who found Dorr's lifeless body—grown thin and sharp of temper with the passing years, rode up to the house. The varying fortunes of the range had brought him the foremanship of the Circle-Z some three years back. That he still officiated in that capacity, will—to the initiated—be proof enough of the quality of his performance.

Naturally, Race came and went at his own pleasure. For the last few days he had been absent on one of his regular inspections of the

Circle-Z outposts. A long conference with Thad always came as a matter of course after these trips, but the old cowman appeared particularly annoyed at seeing him enter the house this morning.

Race's face was unruffled as ever, but his horse bore signs of a hard ride; and Thad knew that beyond a doubt the man had come from as far as Kelly Creek, otherwise he would have ridden in the preceding night. In truth, Race had left Kelly Creek at a few minutes to four that morning. All of which said that something was amiss, and Thad was in no mood to discuss the affairs of his ranch this morning.

The foreman nodded as he entered the room. He did not expect to find the old Basque there, and he stared at him questioningly.

"Thought you was alone," he said then, addressing Thad; "Got to see you."

"You'll have to wait," grunted Thad, his mouth full of food. "I'm leavin' here directly."

Race was not to be dismissed so easily. He said bluntly:

"I broke my neck gettin' here. It's important. I got to see you before you go."

"And I tell you you can't!" Thad declared vehemently. "I got worries enough without listenin' to yours. You're the foreman of this outfit. Do somethin', if somethin's wrong."

Race started to protest, but Thad cut him short with:

"I ain't a-goin' to listen to you! You see me when I git back."

"All right," Race said tartly. "I'll speak to Miss Necia." He started for the door, muttering under his breath: "She's the real boss of this outfit, anyhow."

Thad heard him. His face reddened, and he winced.

"Hey!" he cried. "You needn't go lookin' around for Necia; she ain't here."

Race stopped and came back.

"Pretty early for her to be off," he grumbled.

"She wa'n't here last night neither," Little Billy put in from the kitchen doorway.

Thad reached for a cup, and with the evident intention of hurling it at his cook he got halfway to his feet.

"Git!" he roared, and Little Billy disappeared. Thad expected Race to ask questions. Instead of doing so, however, Eagan said flatly:

"All right! It's up to me. Our stuff comes out of the hills this morning."

Both Thad and Angel got to their feet at this. Thad's face actually went white beneath its tan.

"What?" he gasped. "What do you mean?"

"Just what I said," Race answered grimly. "There ain't a thing left below Kelly Creek. It's all burnt to the roots."

Thad's mouth sagged as comprehension came.

"Cows are turnin' off their calves," Race went on, taking a savage delight in the old man's interest now in what he had to say. "They can't feed 'em. I counted sixteen dead ones yesterday. Another ten days of this and we'll never get a head fat enough to ship this fall. Maybe we won't have anythin' left to ship."

A groan escaped Thad as he sank back into his chair. He glanced at Angel as if asking him what was to be done.

"The drought," Angel muttered, and Thad thought to himself:

"Yes; I laughed when that ragged fool stood here and told me it would come. God! How'd he know; how'd he know?"

Aloud he said: "You can't turn our stuff on the hay-land, Race. What'll we do this winter without hay?"

"We won't need any hay this winter if we can't get grass this summer—this week. I tell you you could play a tune on the slats of our stock. They've got to come down to the meadow-land.

It ain't none too good, but it'll save 'em for a while."

"But it can't be so bad north of the creek," Thad said, his tone almost a question.

"It'll be bad soon enough." Race paused and looked away. He could see Thad aging before his eyes. He was glad Necia was not there. His news would have worried her. He was surprised to hear Thad say:

"Don't say anythin' to Necia about this when she gits back. You understand?"

Race nodded. He knew how hard it was going to be to keep it from her.

"I'll start movin' them to-day," he said.

He went out then. Thad heard him stop to turn the windmill rudder; cursing the while at finding the wheel idle.

The horses which Thad had ordered were outside. They nickered impatiently, but Thad only sat and stared at Angel. Even now he could hardly believe that the blow had fallen. He wondered how Joseph had known that the drought would come. Did he know other things as well? Was it as Angel had said—had the boy some sort of power?

Thad had felt the Circle-Z sufficient unto itself. How many years had it been in the making? "God!" he muttered, shaken by the realization of how long it had taken him to build it into the formidable business it had been only a few yester-days ago. To himself he said:

"I ain't a-goin' to lose it. It can't be. How can the little fellows stand out, if I can't? I got cash. I'll lease some range."

But where?—up north? Perhaps it had been leased already. Why had he waited? Anyhow, he was safe for a month. He had hay-land enough to last him that long.

"It's got to rain," he thought. "A month—" and then he knew that it would not rain—not enough to matter. Hay had sold for forty-five dollars a ton one winter. What would it bring with less than none in sight?

He pulled at the neckband of his shirt as if it were tightening about his neck like a noose. When winter came, he had to have hay. Many tons of it!

A flock of crows cawed their way over the house. Thad shuddered. Had the crow told Joseph the drought would come? Insane hatred of the boy blazed in him.

An hour ago he had scoffed at Joseph; now, with equal certitude, he credited him with having brought the drought. He had mocked the boy's companions—Grimm, the crow, and Slippy-foot, the coyote—but as he saw them now in his mind's eye a feeling of dread gripped him. Fit mates were they for the one whom they followed.

Things of evil; creatures of ill omen moving in the shadow of death. Where death came, they grew fat. They were the great pariahs, the outcasts of the desert. And the hell-spawned creature who consorted with them was their blood brother!

The lust to kill mounted in Thad. He thought of Necia and how Joseph had stolen the love that had been his. He no longer doubted that this had happened. Nothing else could explain her conduct. Everywhere he turned, ruin faced him. In every direction, Joseph Gault arose to menace him.

A fly buzzed about his bald head. He raised his hand and killed it as he would kill that other thing. An unintelligible grunt burst from him. He got up hurriedly. Angel's eyes were on him. He read fear in the Basque's gaze.

What were the sheepmen going to do? Humph! He didn't care what they did. Sheepmen brought trouble wherever they came. But for this one, Joseph Gault would not have come back. This Basque was at the bottom of it! A savage strain in Thad flashed to the surface, and he laughed contemptuously at Angel.

"You're shakin', ain't yuh?" he cried. "You

know the dose I jest got is a-comin' to you. Ain't nothin' a-goin' to stop it. You're a-goin' to be cleaned out jest like the rest of us." Thad chuckled mercilessly and said:

"The Gaults has got even at last."

He stepped into his bedroom. When he came out he held his rifle in his hands.

"Come on!" he exclaimed. "I'm a-goin' to git him."

CHAPTER XXIII.

"LEAD THE WAY!"

THEY said no word to each other as they rode
along. The sun climbed high. Heat waves
danced across the valley. Thad's rifle barrel grew
hot to his touch. The trail began to swing up-
ward; their horses' hoofs thudding dully in the
deep dust of it.

Thad, grim and uncommunicative, led the way.
Angel followed him at the distance of a horse's
length. Between them was no longer any common interest. Each passing second only emphasized this the more, for as they continued to climb
a great change came over the Basque.

Angel's set expression left him. Little by little
he straightened until he rode erect. A weight
seemed to have been lifted from him. His eyes
lost their fevered brightness. The shoulders that
had sagged with defeat were now thrown back.
His lips parted as if with the eagerness of some
sudden desire.

He urged his horse ahead until its nose was at
the other animal's tail. He had been a laggard

—listless, making each turn of the trail with drooping spirit—but he was alive now; anxious, impatient at the pace Thad set.

At this moment he was the more courageous of the two, and this had not been so back at the ranch. Since dawn he had been setting his house in order. His task was well-nigh finished.

He had dealt so long in pride that he did not know how ennobling humility was. So he did not suspect that his present exhilaration was due to the fact that he had gazed on himself as he truly was—a grasping, narrow-minded bigot—and been ashamed. No less was true, however, and the peace he knew now would not have been possible otherwise.

Thad's rifle began to fascinate him. No matter how often he looked ahead for some sign of those for whom they searched, when his eyes came back to his companion, they focused on the shining gun.

Thad did not look back, but the set of his shoulders told Angel something of the frenzy that gripped the man. The look on Thad's face would have confirmed the Basque's worst suspicion; killer was written in every line of it.

As a younger man, Thad had ridden out after horse thieves and rustlers. Guns had spoken; death had followed as a matter of course, and not always had it been the pursued who died. But that was in the rules of the game; quickness of finger and eye being in no way restricted to the righteous. Thad and the others had made light of those excursions, but their faces had belied their lightly flung talk.

And so it was this morning. Had Kit Dorr been alive to gaze on him he would have seen Thad as he had looked on those now forgotten jaunts, except that the light which burned in Thad's eyes to-day had more of blind rage and less of cunning in it than Kit had ever seen.

Angel knew that, whatever the outcome of their mission, Thad and he were done with each other. He held the man a head-strong fool even in his sane moments. That he was mad now and ready to kill on sight, was plain to Angel. He eyed the rifle intently, almost tempted to grab it out of Thad's hands.

Soon the trail widened, and Angel forced his horse alongside the other. He saw how lightly Thad held the gun—ready to throw it up to his shoulder and fire without warning—and he hesitated about reaching out for it.

They neared the coulee shortly. A coyote flashed across the trail. Thad's rifle came up.

"It is Joseph's coyote!" Angel exclaimed. "Don't shoot!"

But Thad's finger was at the trigger. Angel's hand shot out and knocked the rifle down, the bullet plowing into the ground. Thad wheeled on him, his body shaking as with palsy. For a moment he could not speak so great was his fury.

"It was *his* coyote," Angel repeated. "You would accomplish nothing by killing it."

"Am I takin' orders from you? Am I?" Thad screamed, his voice breaking in its intensity. He saw Angel raise his hand bidding him be quiet. It was the very gesture one uses to a child. Thad's face purpled.

He pulled up his horse and scanned the mountain-side, determined to kill the animal now if it were the last act of his life. A movement in the brush into which Slippy-foot had disappeared caught his eye. He sighted his rifle on the spot, and as he did so, Andres stepped into view.

The big fellow was bareheaded, his tanned chest bared to the sun. Nature had cast his face in a crude mold, his mouth too heavy and his eyes too small, but a sublime fire now had touched Andres, softening his ugliness and endowing him with something of the majesty of a prophet.

Thad lowered his gun as he stared at him, dumfounded at the change in the man. Andres's father was hardly less startled. They held their tongues as the big fellow walked toward them, Slippy-foot at his heels. Why ask what had happened? The light in Andres's eyes was explanation enough.

"Where's my girl?" Thad demanded huskily as Andres reached his side.

Andres fixed his eyes on Thad before he spoke.

"She ees on top the mountain looking down on theese—on theese—wretched valley," he said, quoting a phrase he had heard Necia use. "She ees very happy."

Thad's head jerked back.

"Happy, eh?" he growled. "I'll find that out! And him—where's he at? I want to see him."

"He ees weeth her," Andres replied, a faint smile on his lips as he thought of Joseph and Necia.

"I have been wait' for you. I expect you come. Eef you come in peace, all right; eef not, no; you cannot go on."

"You tellin' me I ain't a-goin' on?" Thad roared. "You tellin' me my business?" A wild laugh distorted his face. "Humph! Let go my horse! You damn traitor, I ain't forgettin' how you fooled us. Take you hand off that horse!"

Andres shook his head.

"No," he said. "You do not forget, eh? Me, I not forget either. I remember you offer me lots of money if I keel Joseph." He paused until he was sure Thad understood what he inferred.

Then: "Mebbe I never forget that, *señor*. Eet depend on you."

Andres had taken hold of Thad's rifle. The old man tried to yank it out of his hand.

"I take those gun," the big fellow said evenly, his spirit unruffled.

Andres had the rifle by its barrel, his huge hand holding it as if it were in a vise. Thad grunted as he struggled with all his might to drag the gun away from him.

A peculiar glitter, as cold as ice, came into Thad's eyes as he noticed that the muzzle was pointed at Andres's breast. His hand dropped back to the trigger, the blood left his face; he caught his lower lip between his gums and drew it in until his chin was as tightly drawn as the head of a drum. His nostrils quivered as a wolf's does when it snarls.

Angel was alive to what was happening, but before he could reach out to knock the gun down Andres's wrist turned. The rifle popped out of Thad's hands, but his finger had pressed the trigger. The rifle roared.

Angel groaned, expecting to see his son fall. The bullet had not touched him, however, and he merely stood and shook his head reprovingly at Thad.

"Theese gun ees very bad theeng *señor*," he

said slowly. "They make much trouble."

Thad grew limp in his saddle. Dully he saw Andres unload the rifle and toss the cartridges into space.

"I am not angry weeth you," he heard Andres say. "You are not yourself. I have used a gun, too; eet proves nothing. You theenk you have been wronged. Eet ees not so!"

Andres stepped aside that Thad might pass, and turning to face Angel, he said in Basque:

"And now you, my father, must hear the truth from me. I told you that I would do something for the Irosabals. Well, I have done so. I have made my peace with him. He knows! Margarida did find Timoteo. Joseph knows the truth! But he has taken my hand. We are friends.

"You are an old man, my father. I am your eldest son. Soon I will be the headman of my clan. I have raised my hand to God that when that day comes I will undo all that you have done. You have taught us to hate. You have led us far from our neighbors. You have done everything you could to hurt Joseph. You drove Margarida away for no reason at all; and now we suffer. The day may not be yet, but even now we must walk apart. You bow your head as if ashamed of me. Well, it must be. I—I am right with myself at last. When I left you last night, I knew I should do as I have done."

Angel raised his hands in supplication as his son finished.

"No, no, Andres!" he cried. "You have no need to feel ashamed. I have been a misguided man!"

Thad raised up to stare at Angel. He saw something of the divine fire that had touched Andres in the father's eyes. He gripped the pommel of his saddle to steady himself.

Andres could marvel too. Was this the father he had known? Newly found affection welled up in him.

"God has done this," he thought. "Joseph was right."

He saw his father's lips tremble.

"God forgive me!" Angel cried. "My Margarida!"

It was the first time in twenty years that he had uttered that name. He called to her again in Basque, asking mercy.

Andres placed his hand on his father's shoulder, but Angel threw it off, engulfed in contrition. His parched soul was not to be denied now that the spring of penitence had begun to flow. He seemed oblivious of Thad as he poured out his remorse.

Thad stirred uneasily in his saddle, perspiration not due to the blazing sun dampening his brow. There was too much talk here of God for him.

Angel's emotion only confirmed an opinion Thad had long held of the Basques. In his youth he had considered them a sentimental, zephyr-swayed race with no more dependability than the Mexican possessed. The torrent of words which Angel poured forth convinced him that he had judged them correctly.

He was even glad that he stood alone now. He asked himself why he had ever consented to having anything to do with them. He had got along without them for years. That water-right—he hadn't needed the money. Hell! What a fool he had been!

He curled his lips as he turned his eyes on Andres. The booby! He was sorry he had missed him. Well, he would go on alone. He had come for Necia, and he wasn't going back without trying to get her. Let these boscos tear their hair and cry out to God if they wanted to. He wasn't any fool! Courage, of a sort, came to him.

"Where's he at?" he demanded of Andres. "I ain't interested in hearin' any more of your singin'. I want to talk to my girl. Where's this Joseph?"

Andres's eyes lifted at Thad's insulting tone. Angel saw his son's frown.

"He does not matter," the father said in English; "he is as guilty as I. He offered hate and I gave hate. Pay no attention to him, Andres. We are done with returning injury for injury. If he will follow, let him come.

"Lead me to Joseph. I know no harm has come to this man's child.

"But I am ready to go. Take me to him. I want to get down on my knees to my grandson. I would that I had other sons as noble as you and Joseph, Andres. Go! Lead the way!

"And I say to you now, Andres, that although my flocks are menaced and my crops are dying in the fields, that if I save them—that if somewhere in the north we can find range to keep my stock alive—that Joseph shall share alike as one of my own.

"I denied his mother, I ruined his father and I reviled him. But if I can repay, I will—to the utmost! Let this man have his horse. Here—" He dropped the reins over the animal's head and swung himself to the ground, exclaiming:

"On foot, my hand in yours, Andres, I will go on! And if this man follows us, let him come in peace."

Andres started on, his father at his side.

Shortly they came to where they could look down on their home, a white mote swimming in a sea of brown.

"See!" Angel murmured. "Our home! Even the poplar leaves are turning yellow. They need water as my soul needed tears.

"Joseph has looked on that *caserio* when it was green, when it was the home of abundance. It may never be again. But be it what it will, it shall be his home. He shall share it with me.

"And if he loves this girl, Necia, she shall come, too, for she is worthy of him."

Andres nodded, and as they turned across the coulee he glanced back to see old Thad following them on foot.

CHAPTER XXIV.

MY HOUSE SHALL BE YOUR HOUSE.

SINCE dawn Joseph and Necia had rested on the mountain-top. She had won from him the story of the message his mother had carved there and she had insisted on paying such tribute as she could to the memory of her whose faith was an inspiration.

Grimm had looked on solemnly as the girl knelt in prayer. A flock of his curious fellows had wheeled above him, but the great bird had not heeded their cries. Something of the peace which touched Joseph seemed to have come to him, and as Necia raised her hands to call down a blessing on Margarida Gault, he closed his eyes as if concurring with her.

From the elevation where Joseph and Necia stood they could see far across Nevada. To the north, rose the brown hills of Oregon through which the Owyhee flows to the Snake. Beyond these hills, and to the west, lay Malheur County with its life-saving lakes. Somewhere in that country Joseph knew his father stopped.

Peter Organ knew that land too. Word must be sent to Peter. He could be depended on to find the man who held the fortunes of Paradise in his hand. Andres must go. Less than a day's riding would bring him to the Pingree ranch.

Joseph reasoned that if his father were not hard to find, he might hope to see him here on Buckskin by evening of the following day. And every day counted now.

Whatever gladness he felt in looking forward to seeing his father was tempered by a questioning of his own ability to convince him that the Basques should not suffer for what Angel had done. He knew that it would be no easy task.

Joseph had not arrived at any definite plan regarding his own procedure; nor could he well do so until he had talked with his grandfather. He knew that must be his first move, and if the Basque would not come to Buckskin, he must go to him.

Not that Joseph hoped for any coöperation from Angel. He still held that to expect aid from his grandfather was to tempt fate. But, once for all, he must know where the Basque stood. On what he took away from his meeting with the man should depend his future action.

He had told Andres about his father, but he had sworn him not to reveal a word to any man, for Joseph had no thought of bribing the people of Paradise into accepting him by holding out a promise of what his father would do for them. Before he said any word to his father the Basques and their neighbors must show him that they were ready to bury their old quarrel.

He realized that he had a powerful aid in Andres, but Angel's grip on his people was strong. Joseph wondered if they would desert the father for the son.

And Thad Taylor—? Joseph knew he could depend on him to try to frustrate any move he made. In this, he was swayed by the belief that Thad's enmity to him was only the beginning of a repetition of what his father had gone through with Angel. He accepted it as such, and as his arm tightened about Necia he found the price not too high. Come what would, they belonged to each other. Something of his thought crept into his eyes and Necia lifted her lips and kissed him.

He held her close, gazing into her eyes, realizing anew the wonder of her.

"You are quite happy, Joseph?" she asked softly.

"Happier than I had ever dared to believe I would be. Bitterness is gone from my heart. I pray that I may give others some little part of what you have given me. I shall make them no promise, but if they show me that they are willing to help each other I shall leave nothing undone to aid them. I have decided to send Andres for my father. Before he comes, I must go to the valley."

"I will go with you, Joseph," Necia murmured. "If grandfather has talked—"

"Do you think that he has?" Joseph interrupted. "He will hesitate long before he does, because he must know that it will not be easy for him to make any man who knows you believe anything evil of you. From what you have told me I can see that he will hesitate to ask even his own men to aid him.

"And he can not strike me without hurting you. Already, you see, you safeguard me, for he can not explain his own position without telling some part of the truth; and that he will not do.

"But you shall go with me. Your grandfather may try to prevent you from marrying me; but we shall not wait."

Necia felt his arms tighten and she looked up after a moment, her words merry on her lips:

"But you have not asked me to marry you, Joseph."

"No?" he smiled back at her. "Is it necessary?"

Necia shook her head naïvely and brushed his cheek with her lips.

"No," came her muffled answer.

Grimm's eyes had grown large at what went on before him and neither Joseph nor Necia heard him beating his wings. When Necia looked up, Grimm was gone.

"Grimm?" she questioned. "He was here a moment ago."

Joseph glanced below them, surprised that the crow had left without calling. He was about to say as much to Necia when he saw Andres coming up the trail, his father at his side. Necia saw them at about the same time.

"There is Grimm," she said, "perched on Andres's shoulder."

Joseph did not answer, for he saw how father and son walked hand in hand, and as they neared him his amazement grew. He could not take his eyes away from Angel. Some subtle alchemy had transformed his dour face. He walked with springy step. There was color in his cheeks.

Here was a miracle come to pass! Some sixth sense whispered to Joseph, and he trembled as he glimpsed the truth. Could this be? Had the impossible happened?

He gazed again at his grandfather. A glad

cry broke from him. He raised his hands and stepped forward to meet him.

Angel did not hesitate. He caught his son and bade him wait; alone he came to Joseph, his face working nervously as he fought to control himself.

"Joseph!" he cried. "My Margarida's boy!" His voice broke completely. A sob shook him as he sank to his knees. Unintelligible Basque words flowed from his lips. They were not meaningless to Joseph, for their import was plain.

The boy's throat went dry as he gazed down on the man at whose hands he had suffered so long. He had not been prepared for this moment and his effort to appear calm cost him dearly.

He marveled that he could look on his grandfather without rancor. Subconsciously he wondered what had worked the miracle which he beheld.

Andres's hand must have been in it. And Andres——? Joseph was doubly overwhelmed as he thought of the change in the big man.

And Necia had said this would happen! Now, indeed, was there a chance for him to succeed. A whole people were to be delivered from the prejudice that had dwarfed them!

Times without number he had thought of the day when his grandfather should stand before him crushed. A savage joy had always been his at the contemplation, but the gladness that was his now made the memory of that pleasure mean and small.

Joseph wished that his father could have stood there at this moment. For close on thirty years the breach between the Gaults and the Irosabals had been widening. In a way life had been pointing to this hour. Here was the turning point. The suffering and misery of those wasted years was being expiated now.

Studied injustices that he had once held unforgivable seemed less cruel as he listened to Angel's repentance. For good or evil, the man had always been a force. He had surmounted obstacles that would have defeated any but the hardiest. Beyond doubt he had asked more of himself than he had of his sons.

Andres and the others had been satisfied with a smattering of English; the father had not stopped there. It was a small thing, but indicative of the man's ability to take out of himself whatever he needed.

Joseph dismissed the thought that fear had driven his grandfather to his knees. The man's grief was too sincere to have sprung from any thought of self.

Grimm, the crow, had fluttered to the ground from Andres's shoulder. He came now and stood looking at Angel. Joseph became aware of the big bird as he looked up at him, his great golden eyes seeming to say:

"Be not afraid. I recommend this man to you."

And Joseph hesitated no longer. He placed his hand on his grandfather's gray head.

Necia and Andres had not moved, so completely had they been caught up by the drama being enacted before them. They held their breath as they saw Joseph reach out a hand to Angel.

"Arise!" they heard him say. "'I forgive you. It is not for me to judge you."

Angel clutched Joseph's hand, greedily.

"Can you forgive me?" he cried pitifully. "I—I—how can I ask you to? No, no, Joseph, I dare not. I have been mad! Thirty years—thirty years of bitterness. I—"

Joseph tried to stop him as he scourged himself.

"No," Angel insisted. "My lips have been sealed too long. I have much to say. I have stopped at nothing to injure you and your father. And my poor Margarida! God forgive me! Joseph! Joseph!"

And Angel bared his soul as he had done once before that morning; though rarely has man reviled himself as he did now. With frenzied exactness he recalled every incident of his persecution of Joseph's father and mother. He made himself out a monster, disdaining any excuse for what he had done.

Once again was the story of Kit Dorr's death told. It was as if Joseph listened to the history of his own life, so closely had Angel's vengeance been woven into it.

Joseph did not offer to stop him again. He let him go on until he had quite finished. He stooped then and helped his grandfather to his feet.

"Come—come!" he said. "There is work for you to do. Between us we shall bring a new understanding of life to the people of Paradise. We will bid them hope again. We will show them that they must depend on one another. Prejudice must go. Good-will must take the place of hatred and suspicion.

"And we will go to them together. We have been enemies; they shall see us friends."

"Friends?" Angel echoed Joseph's hope. He appeared to doubt that this could be.

"We shall be friends," Joseph repeated. "It is God's wish. There is suffering in Paradise. Mountain and valley know now that I spoke the truth; the lean years are here. Now must men who have been enemies take each other's hand and share what remains to them.

"Where there is water, no man shall be denied. The rich must help the poor. From day to day the famine must be put off. Even so, there will not be water enough for all. Each must be satisfied with less than enough.

"Some men will say: 'I will not share with my brother. Alone, I may withstand the drought, together we all shall fail.' And these will we find hard to convince, for there is truth in those words. We *may* fail. Faith, alone, must sustain us."

"Let me be the first, then, to prove that it is enough," exclaimed Angel. "We can not save our crops, but we can keep our stock alive. I will close my irrigation ditches to-night. Let those men whom I have despoiled divide the water that I will turn back into Martin Creek.

"Below the Reserve there is fall grazing-land on which I have always fattened my sheep. Let my neighbors lead their stock there. Let them share it among them. And all my people shall share what they have with their neighbors.

"You shall be able to say unto all men that the Basques are their friends. I stole this mountain from your mother. I return it to you now, and what I have undone here shall be restored tenfold."

"But I ask nothing for myself," Joseph said humbly.

"No; it is I who ask, my son. Come to me and let me put my arms around you. I have said to Andres that my house shall be your house. As one of my own you shall share. In my old age will I try to do for you what the father I robbed you of would have done."

"But my father lives!" Joseph exclaimed. "He is not far away."

The news staggered Angel. Joseph caught him as he thought he was about to fall.

"Bring him to me," the old man murmured weakly. "Let me see him, Joseph. Let me speak to him. I know he can not forgive me, but I would speak to him."

"Grandfather, I can not make any promise for my father. It is for you to make your peace with him. He is in Malheur County. I was going to send Andres to Peter Organ. Peter can find my father."

"Andres has other work," Angel declared. "Come," he said to his son. "I want you to go back to your brothers, Andres. Tell them to come to my house to-morrow. The flocks must be left with the dogs to guard them. In my house to-morrow, I want all of my family. Let no one stay behind."

And then to Joseph he said: "We can telephone to Peter. I will ask him to find your father and to come at once. I will explain to Peter. I will go to the valley and send word to every man to meet at my house to-morrow. And you, Joseph, you will come with me?"

"That I cannot do," answered Joseph. "There is one here who is dearer to me than my life. Where I go, she must go."

"And that is well, my son!" Angel turned to Necia and said:

"Come to me, Necia. I have been a wicked, wrathful man, but my eyes have been opened to my faults. I have made you trouble, but I have brought you happiness, too. Not that any man could have kept Joseph and you apart. You are worthy of him. I have said that my house is his house. It is yours also. Come to me."

Mists swam in Necia's eyes as she saw the old man open his arms to her. Angel was paying as she had told Joseph he would pay. And she were blind had she not seen that the promise she had held out to Joseph was coming to pass.

Slowly she came to the old man. He caught her to him hungrily. Now for the first time did he see the message, black with age, that his daughter had carved on the naked rock. With shaking hands he put Necia from him and turned to Joseph.

"How does this come here?" he asked in quavering tones.

"My mother carved it there," said Joseph.

"Your mother—" Humbly Angel dragged himself to the very crest of Buckskin. He put out his hands and placed them tenderly on the crude letters.

Joseph caught Necia and, with his arm around her, they stood reverently with closed eyes as Angel wept. They heard Andres go to his father's side. The big man said nothing, however, and only his father's grief broke the stillness.

CHAPTER XXV.

"I SHALL GO!"

WHEN they looked up, Thad stood before them. Joseph glanced at Grimm and Slippy-foot, wondering why they had not announced the man's coming, and he was surprised to see them turn away from Necia's grandfather as if he did not exist.

Thad looked old and bent. Necia ran to him and put her arm about him. She felt him lean his weight on her.

"Grandfather," she murmured affectionately.

"I have seen and heard enough," Thad muttered. "You leave me, Necia, for this man? Ain't there any love in you for me at all?" His voice shook with intensity.

"You need not ask that," Necia replied patiently. "Neither need you say that I am leaving you. Rather, grandfather, is it you who leave me. Joseph would be your friend if you would permit him to be."

"I don't want his friendship. I don't want nothin' to do with him, nor with these Basques.

I got along without 'em for years. Why should I throw in with them now? I ain't askin' help. I keep what's mine.

"I tell you, Necia, I ain't a-goin' to give you up, either. I raised you pretty near since you was a baby. I ain't never been much on God, but I been strong on my own kind. You come with me. We'll go home!"

Necia shook her head calmly. He would not understand.

"No, grandfather; I love Joseph and my place is with him. I would keep you both, but since I must choose—I choose him."

Thad recoiled at her words.

"So you think to marry him, eh?" he demanded angrily.

"That is my intention, grandfather."

"Well, it *won't* be! I'll see to that. There won't a Gault come into my family. I ain't done nothin' yet; but you wait! You won't marry him!"

"You hate me so?" Joseph asked.

Thad glared at him, contempt on his lips.

"I despise you!" he cried. "You won't marry her!"

"Temper blinds you," said Joseph. "I wonder how you could prevent my marrying your granddaughter if I chose to do so. A word from me and you would not leave this spot to-day. Take some sense unto yourself! You have ever been a rash man. You were the first to accuse my father, and now you do not hesitate to defame me."

"I was right about your father, too, wa'n't I? Maybe that's why I hate you. And to think of Necia takin' up with you, knowin' what she does."

"You are make another meestake, as usual, *señor!*" Andres exclaimed. "Joseph's father was not on the mountain that night."

"Humph! Took you a long time to find that out, didn't it?"

"Mebbe I have good reason for not say anytheeng. I shot Kit Dorr."

"My God! You?"

Thad gazed helplessly from one to the other as Andres nodded his head, realizing that he had been the last to learn the secret.

"Andres speaks the truth," Necia assured him, her voice tired. "It was so long ago; it cannot matter now. My father shot Timoteo, and Andres shot him. I am afraid it was the sort of thing you always approved of, grandfather."

"Maybe it was," Thad answered sharply when she had finished telling him how her father had died. "Leastwise, a man knew where he stood in those days. Young girls wa'n't runnin' off with every Tom, Dick, and Harry. Now you've got laws and religion! What's it done for you?

"I'm an old man with nothin' else in the world but you. I been workin' for you for years; layin' up a fortune. Now you're leaving me; the drought is burnin' up my range. I ain't got nothin' left. God!"

Thad raised his clenched fists to heaven. "I don't care about the ranch! I can lose it if I have to; but I can't see you go, Necia. I can't!" His voice caught in his throat.

Joseph stared at him with mingled feelings. Necia heard a sigh escape him.

"You love her so much then?" Joseph asked.

Thad's eyes blazed as he fixed them on him.

"Yes; and it ain't the kind of love a young fool dressed in rags offers a girl. Your grandpa is a goin' to take you in now. He's a goin' to put a roof over your head. Well, even so, you ain't done nothin' to make me believe you're the kind of a man a girl could depend on. Why'd your father keep away and leave your mother here to starve? The same blood's in you."

Joseph bit his lips at the accusation. Remorselessly, he said:

"You ought to know why my father could not come back. You ordered your men to shoot him on sight. It is idle to deny it. You have no God, but you have set yourself up as one. You have always been quick to judge your fellowmen.

"I doubt that you love Necia half as much as you think. At least, you shall prove it to me. You despise me, but I will trust you. Because I permit you to, you leave here. Between now and to-morrow noon, you can take whatever steps you choose to prevent me from marrying Necia. That shall rest with you.

"Listen to my offer: you said you could see your ranch destroyed if Necia were left to you. Only she matters. So be it! I feel that God has appointed me to bring a new life to this country. My own happiness must not stand in the way.

"No matter how I suffer, I will not fail these men. They have humbled themselves to me. I have sworn to repay them, and I shall. At noon to-morrow I will lead Necia to my grandfather's house. If you come there prepared to accept these men as your friends, to work with them for the common good—I will go! I will leave here."

"Joseph!" Necia cried, and she ran to him. "No! You cannot do this thing! Where you go, I go, too."

Joseph drew her to him and they gazed into each other's eyes longingly.

"It must be as I have said," he murmured at last. "I swore to you that I would accept what

God sent to me. I will not fail Him nor you, Necia. Let your grandfather do as he will. My mother left a message here on this very spot for me. 'Above all else,' she said, 'be true to yourself.' If you have found me worthy, Necia, it is because I *have* been true to myself. Others have sacrificed for me and now I shall accept my rôle without complaint."

Necia could not answer for her tears. Joseph raised his hand to Andres.

"Go, Andres, for your brothers; you, grandfather, to your task; and you, vain man, to your home. To-morrow at noon we shall come to the valley."

Minutes passed before the sound of their going died away. A white wind-cloud sailed across the sun. Slippy-foot crawled into the shade of the mesquite leaving Joseph and Necia alone with the grieving Grimm.

CHAPTER XXVI.

A SHEPHERD SHALL LEAD THEM.

THAD did not return to his ranch immediately after leaving Buckskin. In fact, it was evening before Little Billy saw him ride into the ranch-yard. Thad had wanted to be alone so that he could think, but such thinking as he had done had not made his course any clearer to him.

Little Billy offered him food, and food was the last thing in the world that mattered to him now; but he suffered the man to pester him as he never had before. Race Eagan came in for a word about the yearlings he had moved that day. Race had slouched out without waiting for any word from Thad.

At supper-time his men looked in at him as they went in to eat. Thad thought they were a sullen lot. Surely they knew there was something wrong.

He wondered if they suspected where Necia was. He could not ask them nor would they question him. They would grumble and mutter among themselves, but at his approach a leaden silence would descend on them.

After supper they stood about discussing something. Thad saw them glance into the room where he sat—watching them, although he tried not to—and he felt the accusing thought in their eyes. He pulled down the shades before Little Billy lighted the lamps.

"Going to be a big meeting at the Basque's place to-morrow," the man announced.

Thad was too tired to answer, but the cook's words explained those glances outside his window. The news of Angel's meeting had come in with a teamster. He wondered what they were saying; he got an echo of their talk immediately for Little Billy, taking Thad's silence for permission to continue, said:

"Guess the Circle-Z will be 'bout the only outfit missin' when the meeting is called."

Thad repeated the words to himself. So they knew! Damn the man's indirection! Why couldn't he come out and say that they didn't want him to go to the meeting and exact the price Joseph had set? Thad understood that they were not thinking of their jobs.

It was Necia they were thinking of. Fools that they were, they would rather see her have Joseph, poor and roofless, than anything he could give her. He felt that he could blame Andres for informing them. It didn't matter.

He would go on by himself. And then he knew it did matter for, as Little Billy went out and left him alone, Thad felt isolated—cut off from the very things that were his own.

Race came in before the cook returned to turn out the lights. It was after ten.

"Men are still waitin' for their money," he said.

"Money?" Thad looked at his foreman for enlightenment.

"Pay-day," Race muttered briefly.

Thad had quite forgotten that it was the last of the month. He nodded to Race and said:

"Right. Got it made out?"

Eagan handed him the pay-roll, and Thad opened his safe and counted out the different amounts due his men.

"Reckon they'll be leavin' in the morning'," Race drawled. "Necia's horse came in to-day. Somebody made it his business to find out what was happenin'. They can't see it your way, so they're through.

Thad did not try to deceive his foreman. The blow hurt, and he showed that it did.

"Men will be cheap soon," he said after a pause. "I'll git along. What you a goin' to do?"

Race finished counting the money Thad had given him before he replied:

"I stay with the brand."

This fealty destroyed whatever reserve Thad had left.

"That's the proof of a man, Race," he murmured. "That's the way I was raised—to stick! To stick to the end! And I got to go on this time. I'm a goin' to throw in with the others—Basques included. The ranch will go to hell. We won't save it, Race, but I'll have Necia. You know how he put it up to me?"

"I reckon so. You couldn't back down."

"That's it! That's it, Race, I couldn't back down. I couldn't go to town and fix things so he couldn't marry her. I couldn't do it after the way he put it up to me. I know he thinks I'm bluffin', but I won't welch. I'm a goin' to that meetin'.

"What water we've got we'll share. Maybe we'll have to let somebody else's stuff come in on the only range we've got left. I won't hold back. I'm a goin' through clean. He won't have no reason to come back on my account."

"And yet he ain't askin' nothin' but what's right," Race said half under his breath.

Thad looked at him for a long time before he said:

"You mean that, Race?"

"Yep! I reckon he's doin' about the biggest thing was ever done for this country. I ain't intendin' to tell you what to do or criticizin' none, but I wouldn't play it the way you're doin' it.

"I ain't up much on love, but what little I know about it has proved to me that it's like water. Dam it up in one place and it 'll break through in another. It's got to git somewheres, and it 'll git where it's goin' in spite of hell. And them what stands in its way gits drowned when the flood breaks loose."

Race got up and Thad let him go without a word, feeling more alone than ever. Morning came and the men left. Thad watched them ride away. He had seen men quit in a body before, but these men had no spirit of hilarity about them. After they left, Little Billy told Thad where they were going.

"Reckon they ain't goin' to let you send Joseph away," he said. "They're goin' up to talk to him now."

Thad got his glasses and followed them as they climbed the mountain. They traveled rapidly, and half an hour after Thad lost sight of them they rode across the coulee.

The partisanship of these cowboys affected Necia visibly.

"But, boys," she exclaimed with trembling lips.

"I cannot let you do this. Not a one of you has fifty dollars in his pocket at this moment. Jobs are going to be very, very hard to find. You must go back."

"Won't go back unless you're goin' back," some one answered. The others agreed with the speaker.

"Well—I—I will be going back, I guess," Necia said sadly, her eyes turned away from them.

Larry Dowd, the youngest of the men, came up to Joseph.

"It's up to you whether the old man gets away with what he's trying to do. All you've got to do is say the word."

"My friends, there is nothing I can say. You cannot help me. Whether I go or not depends solely on Thad Taylor. The decision must come from him."

Larry and the others tried to dissuade him, but in the end they left, knowing that they had failed. Necia cried softly as they rode away.

"Come, Necia," Joseph said to her tenderly, "we must not give way. You must help me to go on. No matter where I go, my heart remains with you. And our sacrifice will not be in vain. Let that console you."

But the moment was too much for Necia. Joseph felt her tremble as she tried in vain to control her grief. His own anguish became almost unbearable as he stood there taking his last look at the spot he had come to love so well.

Slippy-foot had the flock ready to move. Grimm, the crow, sad-eyed and silent, stood looking up mournfully as if pleading with him not to go. Below, the valley spread out brown and withered. Tiny dust-clouds moving along the roads told him that men were gathering at his grandfather's *caserio*. It was time that he and Necia started.

"We must go," he murmured. "Dry your tears, Necia."

She drew him closer to her.

"Joseph," she cried, "my heart is breaking."

"And mine! And yet we must go on. Come, let us kneel here and ask God to give us strength."

Silently they knelt and prayed, and when they had finished, Joseph gave the word, and Slippy-foot started the sheep toward the valley. Necia held out her arms to Grimm, and the grieving bird fluttered into them.

Joseph turned his eyes to the crest of the mountain for a moment. Necia waited for him, and then with her hand in his he led the way down the mountain-side. A chill wind sprang up as they went along. Swallows and thrashers began circling in the air, rising high as each succeeding gust struck them.

Slippy-foot ran back and forth, her tongue hanging out to drink in the refreshing coolness. A rabbit leaped across the trail, its fur fluffy and wind-kissed. Somewhere in the chaparral a plover cheeped. It was as if bird and beast felt a renewing of life in that cold wind.

Joseph gazed off toward the east and found the sky a murky white at the horizon. So do sand storms come to the desert. Joseph quickened their pace. When they came to the foot of the mountain they found Angel and his sons there to meet them.

"And my father?" Joseph asked as Angel approached him.

"He has come, Joseph, but he will not set foot on my land. Peter and he are at Stiles's place. I have talked with him; he understands everything. He wants you. Until he has spoken to you he will not give me an answer."

"Was he surprised to learn of me?"

"Not so much as to find that you and I were friends. He hardly believes it now. But let us go on. Many men have gathered together at my house. Richards and those others who had been leasing the Circle-Z water are there. They have taken my hand. This day will never be forgotten."

"My grandfather—has he come?" Necia asked, her face very white.

Angel shook his head slowly.

"No, he has not come."

Andres, dressed in his Sunday-best, as were his father and his brothers, pointed to the darkening sky.

"We must go," he said.

Joseph looked up at the sun, almost obscured now, although he could see no clouds to hide it. The white collars of the Basques seemed to gleam in the somber half-light that stole over the valley. Little whirlwinds of sand arose funnelwise and went swirling across the sun-baked earth.

Somehow the serious faces of Angel and the others appeared a fitting complement to the tragic color scheme with which the coming storm had painted the forbidding desert. Necia had tossed Grimm into the air, and he sailed against the sky now, a black blot.

Angel put Necia between himself and Joseph, and with their sons following them they started on. Their way led past the Circle-Z and as they came to the corner of it they saw old Thad sitting in his buggy, apparently waiting for them.

He got to the ground before they reached him, and leaving his rig, he came out to meet them. Necia felt Joseph's hand tighten over hers.

"Joseph!" she whispered. A pressure of his fingers told her that he heard. She saw him raise his hand, and they stopped and faced Thad.

"I am here," Thad said, speaking with an effort. "I am ready to join you."

Joseph caught his breath. He stepped forward then and said:

"And I am ready to do as I have said I would do. Give me some proof that you will do as you say."

"You've got to take my word for that. I'll give Richards and the others a new lease on Martin Creek. What water I got in the North Fork I'll share. If the meetin' appoints some one to parcel out the range that we have left, I'll divide what I own."

"And you will live in peace with these people?" Joseph continued, pointing to Angel and his sons.

"I will," Thad declared.

"God's curse be on you if you lie. Where I shall go I do not know, but, be it where it may, if I should hear that you had broken word, I will come back."

"I don't pass my word when I can't keep it," Thad growled. "You'll have no cause to come back on my account."

"I am glad to hear you say so. You have asked a terrible price of me. It is almost impossible for me to forget how dearly I pay; I am only a man. God forgive me if there is any regret in my heart at what I do.

"I have shown you the way, even as God showed it to me. It is for you men, for you, Thad Taylor, and for you, grandfather, to reap the fruit. I shall pass from this valley forever, but if the memory of me and what I have shown you lingers, it will be enough."

"But you will go on to my house for the night, Joseph?" Angel asked excitedly.

"No, grandfather. I will leave you here. See, it grows dark. It may be that you are to be tried anew this day. I commend you to God's care. As Solomon in all his wisdom prayed:

" 'When Heaven is shut up and there is no rain, because they have sinned against Thee; if they pray, and confess Thy name and turn from their sins, when Thou dost afflict them: then hear Thou in Heaven, and forgive Thy people.

"If there be in the land famine, if there be pestilence, if there be blasting or mildew, locust or caterpillar: whatsoever plague, whatsoever sickness there be . . . Then hear Thou in Heaven, and render unto every man according to his ways.'—So must you pray.

"I promised myself that should you men forget your quarrels—if you should show me that you were willing to help each other in his need—that if you should do this without any promise of aid, then would I leave nothing undone to help you.

"Andres knows what I am about to say. It will surprise you. Before this month is over the Reserve will be closed to sheep. The order is signed already."

"But there will be no grass left by the end of the month," Angel declared, apparently not as surprised as Joseph had expected him to be.

"But there are other years to come," Joseph went on. "This order has no connection with the drought. It is my father's doing. He hoped to revenge himself on all the Basques. He has leased many miles of range land in Malheur County. Your people were to pay dearly for it.

"I shall go to him now and beg him to lease his land to cattleman and herder alike, and at a price you can afford to pay. My father will not deny me. Let this be your reward. He will come to you. Think well of how he has suffered at your hands.

"If he shows little confidence in your promises, remember why it is so. It is possible that he may use his influence to have the Forester's order rescinded. That will depend on you. And now, grandfather, I will go."

Joseph opened his arms and embraced the old

man. Andres and Felipe crowded close to shake his hand and show him their hearts were with him.

"I wish you well, my friends," he said to them. "Here is one whom you can serve for me." Joseph's arms drew Necia into their embrace. "Whatever you do for her is done for me."

Necia no longer cried, but her eyes were dull, unseeing. In a daze she spoke to Joseph. He bent his head and kissed her before them all.

"God be with you, Necia," he murmured. He turned away then without saying good-by, and old Thad caught Necia as she swayed back and forth helplessly.

The wind had risen until it blew a gale. Black clouds raced along the eastern horizon now. Grimm had long since come to earth, and he fluttered to Joseph's shoulder as the boy took up his staff and trudged after the sheep which Slippy-foot had already started on their way.

No sound came from the little group that watched Joseph go. Quickly the distance between them widened. Once he thought he heard Necia call his name, but he dared not turn back. A second time he thought he heard her cry—or was it the moaning of the wind as it screamed its way across the valley?

His roving eye caught sight of the men and

women who had gathered at his grandfather's house. They had come forth fearfully as the sky had darkened and Angel had not returned. They stood bent over against the wind, their clothes whipping about them.

A booming as of distant surf reached Joseph's ears. Grimm cawed nervously and jumped down on Joseph's arm, hiding his head beneath his wings.

A calling sound came again, and Joseph strained his ears as he walked on. It was a voice! Thad Taylor's voice! He was shouting to make himself heard.

Joseph stopped and looked back. Thad was running toward him. He saw him half stumble once, but he got up and came on.

"Joseph!" he called repeatedly. "Come back! Come back!"

Joseph stopped, wonder holding him.

"I can't do it!" Thad cried: ". . . I can't let you go! You've got to stay! You've got to come back! I was wrong! I couldn't take nothin' from your father knowin' what I'd done to you. If your father's a-goin' to help me save my ranch, you've got to help me save Necia. She looks like she's dyin'."

The wind whipped the words away from his lips.

"Don't mock me, Joseph! Look at the sky! It's like night. What's it waitin' for? What's it gittin' ready to do? Is it me? Is God gittin' ready to strike me?"

The others had come up and their eyes went wide with fear as they heard Thad cry:

"Hold your lightnin', God! Don't strike me down! I believe. . . . I believe!"

A sob choked him, and he sank to his knees muttering a prayer that only his God could understand.

Something thudded in the dust beside him. Here, there—wherever Joseph looked he saw the dust rise in tiny puffs. Something wet struck his face.

It was rain! . . .

It was rain! It was raining! The dry earth sucked in the big drops hungrily. Slippy-foot barked the joy that was in her. Grimm raised his head to confirm the miracle.

The big drops passed. On their heels came the fine, sod-soaking downpour that gives lives to the earth. Men and women were down on their knees, a prayer on their lips.

Joseph went to Necia and bent over her, so white and still. She smiled at him faintly.

Andres took off his coat and offered it to her,

but she would not have it. This long awaited rain was balm to her skin.

In the hills to the north, thunder roared. Martin Creek, that had been so low, began to rise. Rivulets grew until they raced through the fields to the ditches. The ditches began to overflow. The earth seemed to stir as it felt the life-saving moisture seeping into its veins.

Rob MacMonnies, a dry-farmer from east of town, raised his voice, thick with its Scotch burr, in a brave Presbyterian hymn heard more often in some humble cotter's cabin in the highlands of Perth or Inverness than on the sage-brush plains of northern Nevada. As his great voice challenged the noise of wind and rain others joined him.

That their words were in different tongues, their simple melodies no whit alike, mattered not at all. The joy and thankfulness in their hearts sprang from a common seed that made light of such barriers.

"They are singing, Joseph," Necia murmured. "They know they have been saved."

Joseph stroked the hair back from her forehead.

"They have been saved," he repeated. "God only waited for them to accept Him. There is no need now of asking my father to help them. It seems as if God had but waited for your grand-father's acknowledgment.

"To each it must be plain that as soon as he had found a way to face whatever misfortune the drought brought him that the drought ended. And that way was through faith and good-will.

"These men will not forget. They will thank me, but it is you whom they should thank. I have only handed down to them what you gave to me."

Necia patted his hand. Strength was flowing back into her young body. She smiled up at him.

"Does it please you to think so, Joseph? I can hear you saying to your grandfather, that first time you came to the ranch: 'I am a shepherd!' Your words were truer than you knew. You have led your flock into green pastures, haven't you, dear?"

The light of her eyes lifted him to a strange world. He closed his own, and his spirit soared with hers.

Grimm and Slippy-foot came close, but the man and woman they loved were in a land into which it was not possible for them to follow.

THE END.